Henry Winkler and Lin Oliver

HANK ZIPZER
The World's Greatest Underachiever

Barfing in the Backseat

How I Survived My Family Road Trip

Grosset & Dunlap

Cover illustration by Jesse Joshua Watson

GROSSET & DUNLAP
Published by the Penguin Group
Penguin Group (USA) Inc., 375 Hudson Street, New York, New York 10014, USA
Penguin Group (Canada), 90 Eglinton Avenue East, Suite 700, Toronto, Ontario M4P
2Y3, Canada (a division of Pearson Penguin Canada Inc.)
Penguin Books Ltd., 80 Strand, London WC2R 0RL, England
Penguin Group Ireland, 25 St. Stephen's Green, Dublin 2, Ireland
(a division of Penguin Books Ltd.)
Penguin Group (Australia), 250 Camberwell Road, Camberwell, Victoria 3124, Australia
(a division of Pearson Australia Group Pty. Ltd.)
Penguin Books India Pvt. Ltd., 11 Community Centre, Panchsheel Park,
New Delhi—110 017, India
Penguin Group (NZ), 67 Apollo Drive, Rosedale, North Shore 0745, Auckland, New
Zealand (a division of Pearson New Zealand Ltd.)
Penguin Books (South Africa) (Pty.) Ltd., 24 Sturdee Avenue,
Rosebank, Johannesburg 2196, South Africa

Penguin Books Ltd., Registered Offices: 80 Strand, London WC2R 0RL, England

Doodles by Theo Baker and Sarah Stern

Text copyright © 2007 by Fair Dinkum and Lin Oliver Productions, Inc. Illustrations
copyright © 2007 by Grosset & Dunlap. All rights reserved. Published by Grosset &
Dunlap, a division of Penguin Young Readers Group, 345 Hudson Street, New York, New
York 10014. GROSSET & DUNLAP is a trademark of Penguin Group (USA) Inc. Printed
in the U.S.A.

Library of Congress Cataloging-in-Publication Data

Winkler, Henry, 1945-
Barfing in the backseat : how I survived my family road trip / by Henry Winkler and Lin
Oliver.
p. cm. -- (Hank Zipzer, the world's greatest underachiever ; 12)
Summary: Hank must work on a huge homework packet during a family trip to North
Carolina or he will spend the day with his father at a crossword puzzle tournament rather
than riding roller coasters with his mother, sister, and friend Frankie.
ISBN-13: 978-0-448-44328-7 (pbk.)
ISBN-13: 978-0-448-44329-4 (hardcover)
[1. Automobile travel--Fiction. 2. Homework--Fiction. 3. Family life--Fiction. 4.
Crossword puzzles--Fiction. 5. Learning disabilities--Fiction. 6. Humorous stories.] I.
Oliver, Lin, ill. II. Title.
PZ7.W72934Bar 2007
[Fic]--dc22
2007009836

ISBN 978-0-448-44328-7 (pbk.)   10 9 8 7 6 5 4 3 2 1
ISBN 978-0-448-44329-4 (hc)   10 9 8 7 6 5 4 3 2 1

I dedicate this to every road trip I've ever taken, and to those I dream about. And of course, always, to Stacey.—H.W.

For Trudi Ferguson, my best friend and favorite road tripper, awake or asleep.—L.O.

CHAPTER 1

ROAD TRIP

"ROAD TRIP!" MY FATHER shouted, bursting into the kitchen. He waved his arms around with such force that he knocked over the Raisin Bran and spilled half the box on the floor. Fortunately, our dog, Cheerio, pounced on the Raisin Bran, sucking it up like the vacuum cleaner dog that he is. None of the Zipzers have had to pick up even a speck of spilled food since Cheerio joined our family. However, we do have to walk him more than the average dog.

"Did you hear me, guys?" my dad repeated, like not hearing him was even a possibility. "I've decided to take a road trip! And am I ever excited."

My mom, my sister, and I were sitting at the kitchen table, just finishing breakfast. My dad continued to flap his arms around like a happy chicken. This happy chicken behavior is not like my dad. He's more of an angry rooster type.

"Do we get to go, too?" I asked.

"What do you think?" my sister, Emily, piped up. She likes to answer any question out there, whether or not it was intended for her. That's because she's a fourth-grade know-it-all.

"Emily, I think it's a fair question," I said, answering her with my mouth full of half-chewed Raisin Bran with brown sugar. I made sure to leave my mouth open even after I finished talking, just to give her a good shot of the yucky mess on my tongue. It's a ton of fun to gross her out first thing in the morning.

"Honestly, Hank," she sighed, sounding like my teacher Ms. Adolf, which, trust me, is not a compliment. "Do you think they're going to leave us at home with the TV remote and a stack of microwave fried chicken dinners?"

"Emily, don't even say those words," my mom shuddered. "Frozen dinners are full of additives like BHT and MSG and the rest of the alphabet that isn't good for you."

"Of course we're taking you guys," my dad said. "The trip is planned for next week, during your winter break. And guess where we're going? Here's a clue," he added without waiting for our answer. "It's a fantastic amount of fun."

"Disney World!" I shouted, doing a victory dance around the kitchen. But I never got farther than the dishwasher, because my dad said, "Guess again."

"The Grand Canyon," I guessed next. "Okay, so it doesn't have rides like Disney World, but you can ride a donkey down to the bottom."

"Robert did that last year with his mom," Emily said.

Wait, did I hear her voice get all soft and gooey when she said Robert's name?

Yes, I did. I'm telling you, no one but my totally weird sister could manage to get all soft and gooey over Robert Upchurch, the king of the fourth-grade nose-blowers.

"Did Robert and his mother have a good time?" my mom asked as she got up to rinse a few remaining clods of granola off her cereal dish. No Raisin Bran for her. She's definitely a homemade-granola-goop type of person.

"They did until Robert developed a nasty butt rash," Emily said. "The trip got better when he figured out that if he put a washcloth in his pants, the donkey saddle wouldn't irritate his behind."

Emily's skinny boyfriend using terry cloth to fight a rash on his bony butt is just not a picture I want living inside my brain. Unfortunately, it was already there, so I had to shake it loose as fast as I could. I closed my eyes and filled my head with a picture of a pepperoni pizza. Yeah, that was better. The thought of a hot, sizzling slice of pepperoni pizza calms my brain every time.

"Will you guys stop all this yammering about the Grand Canyon?" my dad said. "We're not going there. Where we're going is even better."

What could be better? A million places raced around in my mind. Sea World. Wild Gator Land. The Baseball Hall of Fame.

"I'll give you another hint," my dad said. "It's in North Carolina."

"Oh, Dad! You didn't!" I screamed. "You got us courtside seats at a University of North Carolina basketball game. You are the coolest! Go, Tar Heels!"

I started my victory dance again, but my mom

put her hand on my arm to settle me down.

"Maybe you should just tell them, Stanley," she said to my dad, "before their expectations get too high." She was looking a little nervous, as if she knew something we didn't know.

"All right, kids," my dad said, putting one hand around my shoulder and the other around Emily's. "The Zipzer family is going on a road trip and heading straight for . . . are you ready . . . fasten your seat belts . . . the Grand National Crossword Puzzle Championship Tournament!"

I involuntarily let out a sound. It was somewhere between a moan, a groan, and a shriek. That was followed by a big silence, and I mean a gigantic one.

"Let me get this straight, Dad," I said finally, "because I think my ears might have gone wacko while you were talking. They think they heard you say that we're going to a *crossword puzzle tournament*. Tell them they're wrong. Please, tell them."

"You heard correctly," my dad said. "Isn't it the most exciting idea?" He looked like a two-year-old who had just gobbled up a big chocolate birthday cake. He was smiling so big, you could see his molars, and that's saying a lot for a guy who is not one of your world-class smilers.

I tried to get my mouth to tell him how great it was, but it just wouldn't cooperate. No words came out. Even my brainiac sister, Emily, was shocked into disbelief. I mean, what's a kid supposed to say when he's told that he's going to spend his winter break at a crossword puzzle tournament?

CHAPTER 2

TEN THINGS TO SAY WHEN YOU'RE
TOLD THAT YOU'RE GOING TO BE
SPENDING YOUR WINTER VACATION AT
A CROSSWORD PUZZLE TOURNAMENT

1. Wow.
2. Oh wow.
3. Wowee wow wow wow. (Hank's note: I'm running out of wows, so I'll have to come up with something else.)
4. Well, at least it isn't a lemon-sucking tournament.
5. Sorry, I'm allergic to crossword puzzles. Last time I tried to do one, my upper lip swelled up so much that I pulled it over my head and wore it like a hat.
6. Excuse me? What did you say? I can't hear you. My ears have suddenly turned into cauliflowers.

7. I'd love to go, but I get panic attacks in large crowds of nerds who enjoy writing letters in thousands of little boxes.

8. I have a policy that I only do crossword puzzles on the last Thursday of months beginning with X or Z.

9. I can't make it because I'll be hibernating all winter, since I'm half polar bear on my mom's side.

10. Okay. What's number ten? I can't think of number ten. Let's face it, you wouldn't be able to either if you just found out that a crossword puzzle tournament was in your future.

CHAPTER 3

THAT LIST REALLY came in very handy. In fact, I used numbers one, two, and three on my dad right away.

"Wow," I said to him. "Oh wow. I mean, wowee wow wow wow."

That pretty much did it for the wows, and they seemed to satisfy my dad. He pulled up a kitchen chair and poured himself some Raisin Bran. All you could hear was the clock ticking on the wall above the stove and my dad crunching on his cereal. He liked to eat it before the milk made it into mush.

"You kids are in luck," he said, breaking the silence. "When I saw that the crossword puzzle tournament fell during your winter vacation, I said to myself, this is the chance of a lifetime for a great family road trip. Don't you agree, Hank? Can't you just feel the buzz of excitement?"

"It sounds really . . . uh . . . let's see . . . um . . . it sounds . . . uh . . . really stimulating, Dad. If you're a crossword puzzle fan, that is."

"And who isn't?" my dad asked.

Is he kidding? I can't even spell "neighbor" without mixing up the "i" and the "e," let alone figure out a nine-letter word for a monkey's belly button. All those downs and acrosses make my eyes spin. Of course, my eyes spin when I'm just reading a regular book. I think it's fair to assume that a guy like me, with learning differences up the wazoo, is probably never ever going to shake hands with a crossword puzzle.

"You know, Dad," I said, clearing my bowl and putting the box of cereal back on the shelf in the pantry, "it just occurred to me that sometimes I get carsick on long trips. I'm thinking that to be sure I don't mess up the upholstery in the minivan, maybe I'll call Frankie and ask if I can stay with him."

"But you'd miss the crossword puzzle tournament," my dad said. "Hank . . . it's the Grand Nationals."

I didn't know how to tell my dad that I wasn't exactly thrilled to watch a bunch of older folks pushing their mechanical pencils around a cross-word puzzle for a couple of days.

"Hank," my mom said, "I've done a little research on the Internet, and I found out that within a ten-minute drive of Dad's tournament is some kind of roller coaster park which is supposed to be quite famous. The Colossus something . . . I forget the exact name."

My world came to an immediate stop.

"Mom, you're not talking about Colossus Coaster Kingdom in North Carolina, are you?"

"Yes, honey, that's exactly the name of it. You know about it?"

"Are you kidding? Colossus Coaster Kingdom is world-famous. It's got the seven biggest roller coasters in the whole United States. It's the home of the Howling Tornado, the Tower of Fear, and the Super Duper Looper!"

"I'm getting nauseous just thinking about them," Emily said.

"That's because you don't appreciate the fine art of roller coaster riding," I snapped at her. "Did you know that the Super Duper Looper turns you upside down seven times within thirty-seven seconds?"

"Like you even know how long the ride is," Emily said.

"I know that it wouldn't make me throw up, unlike someone I know who tossed her cookies on the Camp Snoopy baby train at the Long Island County Fair."

I knew that would make her mad. Emily hates to be reminded that she's a barfer.

"Hey, I couldn't help it," she said, her face turning all red. "I had just eaten a hot dog and had a poor reaction to the very sour sauerkraut, which has been proven to be a highly difficult food to digest."

"Would you like to have a chance to ride those roller coasters, honey?" my mom asked me.

"It would be a dream come true," I said, and I meant every word.

"Well, Hank, here's your opportunity," my dad added.

"This is so cool. Frankie loves roller coasters and he's going to be *so* jealous!"

"Tell them the best part, Stanley," my mom said with a smile.

"Your mother and I have decided that each

of you can bring one friend on the road trip!"

"I'll call Frankie!" I dashed for the phone. Suddenly I stopped. Frankie Townsend was my best friend, but my other best friend was Ashley Wong. What if she wanted to go, too? How could I choose just one?

"Wait a minute. Maybe I'll call Ashley. No, Frankie. No, Ashley. No, Frankie. I don't know who to call."

"Let me stop you before your brain fries," Emily said. "I happen to know that Ashley is going to soccer camp at the Y over winter break. She told me that when we were riding up in the elevator yesterday. So she couldn't go, anyway."

"Wow, that takes the pressure off. I'll call Frankie."

"And which friend are you going to bring, sweetie?" my mom asked Emily.

"My best friend in the whole world," she answered.

"Oh no, not Sally Dink Dink," I said. "She smells like stinky cheese."

"First of all, her name is Sally van Oberdink," Emily snarled. "Her grandparents are Dutch."

"Oh, that's where the cheese comes in." I laughed. I have no idea what that meant, but it tickled me to no end.

"And second of all, she is definitely not my best friend," Emily went on, ignoring the fact that snorty little giggles were coming out of my nose. "But we know who is, don't we? And here she comes now."

I heard a scratching on the yellow linoleum kitchen floor and looked up to see Katherine, Emily's pet iguana, clawing her way over to us, looking very prehistoric.

"Wait a minute, Emily," I said. "I can't believe you're suggesting what I think you're suggesting. You're going to invite the lizard?"

"Her name is Katherine," Emily sniffed. "And you know very well she's an iguana, Hank. She is offended by being called a lizard. Just look at how you made her eye twitch."

Katherine hissed at me and shot her gray tongue out so far it almost touched my new snow boots. One thing you for sure don't want on your new snow boots is reptile saliva. I had the feeling it would eat right through the rubber.

14

"Oh, excuse me, Katherine," I said, jumping back to avoid another attack of iguana-tongue goo. "The word 'lizard' will never come out of my mouth again. It will be replaced by 'the ugly slithering one' from now on."

Just at that moment, Katherine lifted her upper lip, showing a few of her 180 pointy yellow teeth, and hissed again like a hungry snake.

"I think she speaks for herself," Emily said. "Enough said."

"Mom," I pleaded. "You're not really going to let Katherine come on our road trip. I mean, aren't there friend rules? Like they have to have two legs. And hopefully no tail? Oh wait, that would eliminate Emily's other friends, too."

"Well, I don't see why Katherine can't come," my mother said. "She doesn't eat much. She can ride in her crate. And she never argues over what radio station we're going to listen to. What do you say, Stanley?"

My dad wasn't listening. He had picked up the *New York Times* and was busy working on the crossword puzzle as fast as he could. His stopwatch was propped up on the table.

"Stanley, did you hear me?" my mom asked him.

"Yes, Randi. Whatever you say is fine."

"So it's settled," my mom said. "Hank, you'll invite Frankie. And Katherine will be joining us as Emily's special friend."

"And we'll ride roller coasters until we barf to our hearts' content," I added.

I laughed as I headed for the door. Even the idea of seeing my teacher Ms. Adolf at school didn't seem so bad. It's amazing what the thought of roller coasters can do to a guy's mood.

CHAPTER 4

THE GREAT NEWS was that Frankie's mom and dad said he could come with us on the road trip. Well, at first they said no because they wanted Frankie to be home for Christmas. But then my dad worked it out so the whole trip would only take eight days—four days to drive to North Carolina, two days at the crossword puzzle tournament and roller coaster park, and two days to drive straight back to New York. Four plus two plus two—let's see—that is eight days, right? Help me out here, readers. You know I have math issues.

Anyway, the point is, when my dad told Frankie's dad that he could get him home the day before Christmas, Frankie got the big okay. I have to give credit to my dad. He was really trying to make this a great family trip.

Frankie and I spent every night that week

in our clubhouse in the basement of our apartment building, poring over pictures of Colossus Coaster Kingdom. I was drooling over the Super Duper Looper the most. Frankie couldn't choose his favorite, but it was between Freefall and the Stomach Slam. I have to admit, they both looked awesome.

I didn't tell Frankie this, but I was keeping my fingers crossed the whole week that I would meet the height requirement for the roller coasters. When I wasn't staring at pictures of roller coasters, I was in my room practicing standing on my tiptoes so when they measured me, I could eke out every fraction of an inch I have. I even tried wearing three pairs of socks to lift me just a squidge higher on the old Height-O-Meter.

Well, maybe four pairs.

Okay, five, but I promise that was the max. Wearing tennis shoes with five pairs of socks can get a little toasty, not to mention the tightness-around-your-foot factor. I think my toes lost weight.

It seemed like it took forever to get to Friday, the last day of school before winter break. And on Friday, it seemed like it took forever to get to three o'clock. Frankie and I spent the whole afternoon staring at the clock, ticking down the minutes and seconds to freedom.

Eight . . . seven . . . six . . . five . . . four . . . three . . . two . . . one.

Bbrrriiiiiiiiiiiiiiiiiingg! Yay, there it was! The last school bell before winter break. Everyone in class exploded out of their chairs and headed for the door. I threw myself into the crowd, and had the bad luck to get wedged in too close to Nick McKelty's armpit. I don't think McKelty has made contact with water or soap for six months. The smell that came off him actually curled my nose hairs. I could tell because I felt them rolling up and down in my nasal passage. And I'm not exaggerating, either.

"Where are you rushing to, Zipperbutt?" McKelty snarled.

"Only the best road trip ever," I said, being careful to speak without breathing in through my nose.

"A road trip? That is so pathetic," McKelty said. "Me and my dad are taking our own private helicopter to Florida where we're suiting up to be part of the astronaut program."

"That's great, McKelty," I shot back. "Going back to Mars where you came from? I hear being green is accepted there, so you'll fit right in."

McKelty hasn't said one true thing in his whole smelly life. We call it the McKelty Factor, which is truth times a hundred. I'm sure he wasn't going to be in an astronaut program. I'm sure he wasn't leaving New York City. In fact, I'll bet he wasn't even going to leave his La-Z-Boy armchair where he does nothing but sit and eat Ding Dongs and watch the Cartoon Network all day.

I steered by McKelty, making sure I didn't get in his downdraft. One more whiff of him, and I was in danger of my nose actually falling off my face.

"Mr. Zipzer," I heard as I was almost out of the room. "Would you stay behind for a moment?"

My heart stopped. That was Ms. Adolf's voice. What could she possibly want with me? I can tell you this. When Ms. Adolf asks you to stay behind for a moment, nothing good is going to come from it.

"Looks like Zipperbutt's vacation is getting off to a rocky start," McKelty said, walking backward through the door. "Ta-ta, sucker. I'll be watching you from space."

I grabbed hold of Frankie's arm.

"You and Ashley wait for me outside. This will only take a second."

Oh did I wish. I hoped. I prayed.

"No worries, dude," Frankie said. "Ms. Adolf probably just wants to know where you're going for the vacation."

"Or maybe she wants to compliment you on the great job you did on your oral report on how to achieve perfect balance on a scooter," Ashley suggested. She adjusted her glasses, which were decorated with baby blue rhinestones, the way she does when she's worried about something. I could tell she wasn't so sure that I was heading for a compliment.

"That was a cool report," Nico Lubkeman chimed in from where he was standing out in the hall. Nico just moved to my school from California, and he is a great scooter rider. I mean, he's a master on two wheels.

"Thanks, Nico," I said, giving him a big high five. Ashley and Frankie did, too. As my best friends, Frankie and Ashley always look on the positive side for me.

Unfortunately, Ms. Adolf doesn't. As a matter of fact, *positive* was not one of her vocabulary words growing up.

I walked over to Ms. Adolf's desk and waited quietly while she shuffled through the second drawer on the left side of her desk. Or maybe it was the right side. Even under perfect conditions, I can't tell left from right. So I certainly couldn't do it now while I was waiting to see what lousy thing Ms. Adolf had in store for me.

She took out a manila folder that was stuffed with papers. It was about as thick as the New York phone book. When she took out the papers and reached for her stapler, I knew I was in deep trouble.

"Henry," she began. "I have something for you for your vacation."

"Thanks so much for thinking of me, Ms. Adolf, but I'm already packed and I can't fit another thing in my suitcase. Have a great two weeks."

I pivoted on my left foot and tried to take off on my right. Or maybe it was the other way around. The point is, I took off as fast as a bunny going after a carrot.

"Not so fast, young man," Ms. Adolf boomed. I stopped in my tracks, but I didn't turn around. I was hoping that if I didn't look at her, she wouldn't see me.

Good try, but it didn't work.

"Henry, I have prepared a special packet for you, to make your winter break a productive and stimulating one." There are some words that make you feel good all over. Like *home run* or *pizza*. Then there are other words that strike fear in your heart. Like *packet*. I have *never* received a packet that contains anything I would want.

"Inside this packet, Henry, you will find a multitude of very challenging practice exercises in subjects ranging from mathematics to spelling to reading comprehension. All have been designed to help you in specific areas where you need help," Ms. Adolf said. "I know you'll want to thank me for designing this packet especially for you, but there is no need.

Consider it my holiday gift to you." She stuffed the papers inside a manila envelope and handed it to me.

This woman had officially gone over the edge. Thank her? Thank goodness I really didn't have to thank her, because "thank you" was the farthest thing from the tip of my tongue. The things that were on the tip of my tongue sounded a little something like:

Are you totally nuts?

What other kind of gifts do you give—shoes with hundreds of sharp nails glued inside them?

Did you take a special teaching course in how to torture innocent kids?

Instead, I said, "Ms. Adolf, either I just had a really bad daydream, or *you've* just said you're giving me a lot of pages of homework to do on our vacation."

"An hour a day is all it will take, Henry," she said. "That leaves you twenty-three hours for your other amusements."

"But we're going on a *road* trip. With lizards and roller coasters in a minivan stuffed with snacks."

This wasn't my best argument ever, and I knew I was making no sense to her as soon as she said, "That will be all, Henry."

She put on her gray glasses, picked up her gray pen, and began to write gray numbers in her gray roll book. The conversation was obviously over.

This time, the walk to the door was completely different than the first time. I felt like I was walking fifteen miles through sticky tar. When I got out into the hallway, Frankie and Ashley were waiting for me.

"So it wasn't so bad, right, dude?" Frankie said.

"No, Frankie. It wasn't so bad. It was the worst thing to ever happen at PS 87."

"Hank, what are you talking about?" Ashley asked.

"I have two words for you," I said, almost in a whisper. "Homework packet."

"She didn't," Frankie said.

"She did."

"How big?" Ashley asked.

"Nine hundred pages," I said. "And that's just the instructions."

Frankie and Ashley were completely silent. There was really nothing to say except . . . well . . . no . . . there was nothing left to say.

CHAPTER 5

WHEN I GOT HOME from school, I went into my bedroom and noticed that my mom had laid out stacks of clothes on my bed so I could choose what to take on the trip. She had also taken out my special rolly-wheels suitcase with the Mets stickers all over the front.

I closed the door to my room and opened my backpack. I took out the homework packet and put it deep in the bottom of my suitcase. The last thing I wanted was for my dad to see it. It was bad enough I had to do it. I certainly didn't want him making up one of his famous schedules. He loves to do complicated schedules where he writes down how long I should spend on homework assignments. He would be in schedule heaven if he saw that packet.

I piled my underwear on top of it.

Okay, homework packet. Yes, I'm talking to

you. If you want to come along, then you can sit there under my underpants. See how you like that.

Later that night, my grandfather, Papa Pete, came to dinner to say "bon voyage," which he explained to me means "have a good trip" in French.

"Why do you have to say that in French?" I asked him.

"Why not?" he answered.

I couldn't argue with that. Besides, I'm glad to see Papa Pete, no matter what language he's speaking. He's just that much fun.

Frankie came for dinner, too, so my dad could go over the rules of the trip. As we all sat at the table pushing around my mom's Tofurkey Scramble Surprise and other unidentified green and brown foods, my dad ticked off about 112 rules for the trip. The one thing they had in common was that they all started with the word NO.

"No fighting in the car," he said. "No tickling in the car. No asking, 'When are we going to get there?' No whining. No loud music. No trying to recite the alphabet while burping. No passing gas unless it's a matter of life and death."

"You know, Stan," Papa Pete said, trying to get my dad to change the subject, "I'd like to tell the youngsters a little story. Kids, did I ever tell you that I once took a road trip to Maine with my parents, and my father did something I'll never forget? He let each of us choose one place where we could stop along the way."

"What did you choose, Papa Pete?" I asked him.

"A pickle factory outside of Boston," Papa Pete said. "It smelled like garlic and dill and vinegar all rolled into one."

"Eww," said Emily. "How gross."

"It wasn't gross at all, my darling girl," Papa Pete said. "It's the way I hope heaven smells."

Papa Pete and I both love pickles, especially the really sour ones with lots of garlic. We have a pickle snack when we're discussing important subjects.

"I think we should give Dad's idea a whirl, Stanley," my mom said. "Each of us could pick one place to stop along the way."

"Maybe there's a bookstore that specializes in dictionaries," my dad said, taking Papa Pete's good idea and making it horrible.

"Or an organic vegetable farm where we could taste all the young broccoli and Brussels sprouts," my mom chimed in.

"Or an iguana farm where Katherine could visit her relatives," Emily added.

I looked over to Papa Pete for help. What kind of family did I have, anyway? Did anyone in the Zipzer clan know the meaning of fun? Or were they just going to sit there and keep listing the worst places you could possibly go on a road trip?

CHAPTER 6

THE SEVEN WORST PLACES TO VISIT ON A ROAD TRIP

1. A factory where they use visitors to demonstrate how to use dentist drills.
2. A tour of the trash dump where all the world's disposable diapers and Robert's used tissues go.
3. A visit to a school where opera singers learn to break glass while trying to hit their high notes. (I'd have to get earplugs for that.)
4. A factory where they make athlete's foot powder. (Oh wait, maybe that's a good thing because my feet are pretty sweaty in these five pairs of socks.)
5. A guided tour through the publishing plant where they print my math textbook. (I'm getting a rash just thinking about it.)

6. A stop for an afternoon treat at an ice cream store where the only flavor is fried ketchup.

7. A personal visit to the home of Ms. Adolf's twin sister. I don't know if she has one, but I can't even imagine it because the thought of two Ms. Adolfs will do damage to my brain.

8. Oh no, Ms. Adolf's evil twin is still in my brain. How do I get her out? What if she stays there the rest of my life? I've got to stop this list right now and go wash my brain out with soap. Hey, how do I get the soap up there? Maybe through my nose . . .

CHAPTER 7

PAPA PETE'S IDEA caught on right away, and we all became really excited about picking our own place to stop along the way.

My dad got out a whole bunch of maps he had been collecting for the trip and spread them out on the table. We went through them, calling out names of cities and places of special interest, with my dad running back and forth to the computer to look up what we found. Fortunately for all of us, he didn't find any dictionary stores along the route, so he picked the Library of Congress in Washington, D.C. as his choice.

Emily picked the Science Museum of Virginia in Richmond, which we were going to pass right through. Wouldn't you know that little Miss Einstein would pick that for sure.

Frankie, sports fan that he is, picked the University of North Carolina in Chapel Hill as his place, so he could visit the basketball court where Michael Jordan played college basketball.

My choice, of course, was the roller coaster park.

Leave it to my mom to locate an organic honey farm in Virginia where they give tours of their beehives to crazy health nuts like her.

"Did you know that bee pollen is one of nature's most complete foods?" she said after my dad read the description on the Internet of the Buzz Haven Honey Farm and Snooze Inn. "We owe it to ourselves to pay a visit to a bee farm, especially since honey contains so many necessary proteins, vitamins, minerals, and beneficial fatty acids."

"Vitamins, schmitamins," Papa Pete said. "Pollen, schmollen. Give me a good dill pickle any day. One with a real garlic *va-voom.*"

When my dad read that you could stay overnight at the Buzz Haven Honey Farm and Snooze Inn, my mom made him call right then and there to make a reservation.

"Stan," Papa Pete said as my mom brought out dessert. "I have another suggestion to make, if you don't mind my butting in."

"Butt away, Papa Pete," I said, answering for my dad, who was dishing out the Rice Dream Supreme, which my mom actually believes she can pass off to us as ice cream.

"Well," Papa Pete began. "I happen to have read in *Fun Trips for Active Seniors* magazine that there is a stand in Philadelphia called Pat's that sells the best Philly cheesesteak on the planet."

"Way to butt in, Papa Pete!" I yelled. "That can be the family choice."

"Like Mom is really going to eat grilled meat and Cheez Whiz," Emily said, killing the fun as only she can.

"I'm sure I can put something healthy together," my mom answered. "I'll just order a cheesesteak without the meat. Or the cheese. Or the bread. I could always have a nice glass of water and a side of onions."

"Randi, I don't know how you got to be my daughter," Papa Pete said, wiping some Rice Dream Supreme off the tip of his bushy mustache. "The only way I eat grilled onions is when they're smothering a Polish hot dog."

"Well, I wouldn't mind giving a Philly cheesesteak a try," Frankie said.

"So it's settled, then," my mom said. "Everyone has their choice, and the *family* choice will be Pat's."

I was getting to like this road trip more and more. It sounded like it was going to be a total blast. I looked down at the brown, melting lump of I-don't-know-what in my bowl, and even *it* started to look delicious. In my mind, I could see a roller coaster car climbing up one side of the scoop, barely making it to the top, then barreling down the other side. Rice Dream Supreme never looked so good.

"There's one more thing," my dad said, putting down his spoon and clearing his throat. Uh-oh. He had that look in his eye. The look that says, "Warning! You will find no fun living inside me."

"I got a call from your teacher today, Hank," he began. "It seems she's given you a rather substantial homework packet to complete over the vacation."

Ms. Adolf, why are you following me here to the dinner table? Don't you have anything better to do than to make my life miserable?

"Stay cool, Zip," Frankie whispered to me. "And remember to breathe. Oxygen is power." Frankie's mom, who's a yoga teacher, taught him that, and it works for me most of the time.

I took a deep breath, then flashed my dad a very sincere and gigantic smile.

"No problem, dude," I said to him.

I thought my dad's eyes were going to pop out of his head.

"Dude?" he said.

"Dad, I mean. No problem, *Dad*. Not dude. I'm on top of that packet."

"Yeah, but sitting on it doesn't count," Emily piped up. "I saw it lying beneath your underpants in your suitcase. You haven't even opened it."

"First of all, what was your nosy nose doing in my suitcase? And second of all, I only got it today," I snapped. "Just because I'm not like you and I don't do my homework on the walk home from school is no reason to bark at me. That's Cheerio's job."

Frankie and I both laughed. I have to admit, I crack myself up sometimes.

When Cheerio heard his name mentioned, he spun in a circle under the table and started licking my ankle. Without anyone seeing, I slipped him a big spoonful of my Rice Dream Supreme. He barked again, which I think meant, "If you eat enough of it, this stuff starts to taste like chalk."

"Here is my rule, Hank, which is now your rule," my dad said, giving me the big serious stare down he's perfected over the years. "If that packet is not completed by the time we reach the Colossus Coaster Kingdom, there will be no rides for you. Not even the merry-go-round."

"Now that's an excellent rule, Dad," Emily said.

"No, here is an even better excellent rule," I said to her. "Little sisters should keep their mouths shut when they don't know what they're talking about, which is pretty much all the time."

"Hank, don't talk to your sister like that," my dad said. "She's just trying to help you."

"Hankie," Papa Pete said, giving my shoulder a big squeeze. "Just do a little bit every day, and before you know it, it'll be done."

"Easy as pie," I said, flashing a thumbs up to my dad. "I'll be on top of it, don't you worry."

I tried to look confident on the outside. But inside, I had this sinking feeling as I thought about all of those pages of schoolwork. What a rip-off. I was getting no break from homework, even on winter break. This was not a vacation—this was a *workation*.

Oh, Ms. Adolf! Who invited you along on the Zipzer family road trip?

CHAPTER 8

I DON'T KNOW HOW many of you have ever taken a road trip with an iguana in the car, but just in case you ever find yourself in that sorry situation, here's something you need to know.

Iguanas are very fussy about where they sit.

At least, that's what my sister Emily told us the next morning when we were ready to leave.

It was early Sunday morning, and my dad had brought the minivan to the front of our apartment building from the garage where we keep it a couple blocks away. It was freezing cold, so we loaded our suitcases into the back of the car in a big hurry. I couldn't wait to get inside, where it was nice and toasty from the car heater.

"Okay," my dad said once the suitcases were stacked neatly in the luggage compartment.

"Everybody in. Frankie and Hank, you guys sit in the middle seat. Emily and Katherine in the way back."

"That's not going to work for Kathy," Emily said. "She gets carsick in the way back."

"How do you know?" I asked. "She's never even been in the car."

"Oh yes she has," Emily answered. "Remember that time we drove to Aunt Maxine's out on Long Island? Katherine rode in the way back and she turned all green in the face."

"That's because she *is* green," I said. Frankie started to laugh.

"Hank, why don't you and Frankie sit in the way back and let Emily and Katherine have the middle seat," my mom suggested.

"That's not going to work for Kathy, either," Emily said. "There's a draft in the middle seat that comes in through a crack in the window. I don't want Katherine catching a cold and getting a stuffy nose."

"Neither do I," I answered. "If her big snout blows, we'll all get slimed by lizard snot."

"Hey, then Katherine will be just like Robert," Frankie said, laughing so hard he spit out a bite of bagel he was munching on.

"You boys are disgusting," Emily said.

"Oh, and your scaly iguana isn't?"

I looked inside Katherine's crate, just to check. She was just lying there on some clawed up newspaper, munching on a brownish piece of wilted lettuce. Yup, she was still disgusting, all right. No doubt about it.

"Emily," my dad said, getting a little impatient with her, which is something that doesn't happen very often. "Where do you suggest Katherine sit?"

"I think she and I should ride shotgun, next to you."

"Oh no!" I shouted. "That's definitely not happening. If anyone's going to ride shotgun other than Mom, it's going to be me. After all, I am the oldest child."

"I'm making a decision," my dad said, shivering from the cold and pulling his earmuffs down over his ears. "Hank and Frankie ride in the way back from here to Philadelphia. We'll have lunch there, then after lunch, Emily and Katherine will ride in the way back until we get to Washington, D.C."

"I think your father has made a very fair decision," my mom said.

"Fine," said Emily. "You can tell that to Katherine when she barfs in the backseat."

Frankie and I climbed into the way back. Emily got into the middle seat, and put Katherine's crate in the space next to her. My dad started the car and we pulled away from the curb. We were on our way!

"Hey, Em, fasten Kathy's seat belt," I whispered, just to drive my sister crazy. "In case of a sudden stop, we don't want her to get lizardy whiplash."

"Mom, did you hear what he said?" Emily whined.

"I thought I said no whining," my dad hollered from the front seat.

"Hank started it," Emily whined again.

"No, you started it when you invited your four-legged reptile along," I shot back.

"That's enough!" my dad yelled.

And just as quickly as he had pulled out, he steered the car back to the curb. We had gone about ten feet, maybe twenty max. So much for being on our way!

"Everybody out," my dad said, opening the car door.

"But we just got in."

"Stanley," my mom said. "Really, is this necessary?"

"Yes, it is," my dad answered. "I don't want to spend the next week listening to them arguing. Now, if I hear any bickering for the rest of the day, I'm canceling the trip. Do I make myself clear, kids?"

The one thing you can say about my dad is that he makes himself *very* clear. When he says no, he means no. And when he says no bickering, it means keep your lips zipped if you don't have anything nice to say.

We didn't say a word all the way downtown. We rode in total silence. But as we entered the Holland Tunnel, which takes you out of Manhattan under the Hudson River, my stomach growled really loud. Not just a little *grrrrr*, but a long, loud rumbling that sounded like I had swallowed an actual lion. And then a miracle happened. Emily burst out laughing. Then Frankie cracked up and I did, too.

We laughed like hyenas all through the

tunnel, and by the time we came out of it and hit the New Jersey Turnpike, we were having the greatest time in the world.

My mom turned on the radio to her golden oldies station, and started to sing along to "I Can't Get No Satisfaction" in her loud rock 'n' roll voice. Frankie and I joined in, and Emily, too. Get this: Even my dad started to sing. The only one who wasn't singing was Katherine, but I think I saw her blinking her eyes in time to the music.

If you could have seen us, you would've thought, *Now there's one nutty family*. But we didn't care. We were on a road trip, and we were having fun.

CHAPTER 9

PHILADELPHIA DEFINITELY ROCKS. At least the part that I saw.

We got there at about eleven o'clock in the morning. My dad said we should go directly to the Liberty Bell. I was pushing to go directly to Pat's for cheesesteaks, but he said, "Learn first, eat second."

As it turns out, the Liberty Bell is a pretty cool thing to see. It would have been cooler if I hadn't been standing next to my know-it-all sister who blabbed Liberty Bell facts the whole time we were there. Her brain is like a sponge. It just soaks up information and never seems to get full. My brain soaks up information, too, but then it dribbles out like a leaky faucet.

"The Liberty Bell is made of seventy percent copper and weighs over two thousand pounds,"

Emily blabbed as we walked up to the glass building that housed it.

"So does a baby whale," I said. I had no idea if that was true, but let her try to prove me wrong.

While we waited in line, we watched a video that told the history of the bell. It was made in London over two hundred years ago, and was then sent over to America to be hung in the Pennsylvania State House. Hey, I can throw a few facts around, too, if I watch them on a video. When information comes into my brain through my eyes, like when I'm reading, it doesn't seem to stick around too long. But I usually remember most of what I see on TV or hear on a tape.

The video lasted seven minutes, which I know because Frankie was timing it on his digital watch. After it was finished, a guide led us into the room where the Liberty Bell is enclosed in a glass case. Frankie and I moved up real close to get a good look at it.

"Hey, that thing is cracked!" I said.

"If you were watching carefully, you would have learned that the bell cracked shortly after its arrival in America," Emily said. "It was repaired, but cracked again in 1846."

Wow, I guess my mind must have wandered during that part of the video. Oh, yeah. I think it was when those pigeons flew up to the window and were looking in at us. I remember wondering if pigeons are really pigeon-toed.

"Who can read the inscription on the bell?" my dad asked. "Hank, why don't you give it a try?"

There were a bunch of words carved on the bell. I looked at the first one. It started with a P, but after that, I didn't have a clue what it said. I noticed a couple of teenage girls watching me through the glass. No way was I going to mess up in front of them.

"You know, Dad," I said. "I think Frankie could use the reading practice more than me, so I'm going to turn the stage over to him. Take it away, Frankie Townsend."

Frankie knew what I was doing, and like the true friend that he is, stepped right up to help. "'Proclaim liberty throughout all the land unto all the inhabitants thereof,'" he read. "Isn't that what it says, Zip?"

"I couldn't have read it better myself," I said.

And boy, was that ever true.

After we were finished checking out the Liberty Bell, we got back in the car and drove to Pat's. Well, we didn't drive right there. We got lost for about a half an hour first, going up and down narrow streets crowded with red brick row houses. My dad got a little snappy, like he always does when we get lost. My mom kept rolling down the window and asking random people for directions. But before they could answer, my dad would press the automatic window button on his side and roll up her window. He'd rather be lost than ask for directions.

"I know where I am, Randi," he said.

Then he'd drive the wrong way on a one-way street and start tapping his fingernails on the steering wheel. That fingernail tapping is definitely a sign that he's about to blow.

My stomach was screaming for food by the time we finally arrived at Pat's. But within ten minutes, my stomach was one very happy camper. I've had plenty of sandwiches in my eleven years on earth, but this was far and away the best sandwich that has ever made the trip into my little mouth.

It all starts with a big, crusty Italian roll. Then they load it up with strips of delicious beef that has been grilled with a mountain of onions. Then comes the cheese. You can have your choice of American or provolone or Cheez Whiz. I got the Cheez Whiz, just like Papa Pete had suggested.

That sandwich was so delicious that even my mom, who is not an eater of greasy meats, had to take a bite. Actually, she took two bites. Then she broke down and ordered her own sandwich. I'm telling you guys, the Queen of Tofu ate an entire Philly cheesesteak. And licked her chops afterward.

We were all crowded around the little outside table huddled close to the outdoor heater, chowing down on our sandwiches. Even Katherine, in her crate next to Emily's feet, was slurping up a few grilled onions while hissing at the pigeons that were strutting on the sidewalk. I was right in the middle of my sandwich, at the part where all the juices are running up and down your arm, and thinking that this was one of the greatest days of my life, when my dad spoke up.

"So, Hank," he said, rolling up the paper his sandwich had come in. "What's the plan of attack for finishing your homework packet?"

I almost gagged on my sandwich right there in front of all those nice Philadelphia people and their pigeons.

Dad, who talks about homework in the middle of a cheesesteak?

"Can we talk about this another time, Dad? Like, say, never?"

"You've got to tackle some every day," my dad went on, as though he hadn't heard a word I'd said. "You don't want to get behind and then have to play catch-up. That's a serious amount of work you have there."

Boy, he must have gone to a special school to study how to make a guy lose his appetite.

"I promise you, Dad. I have the situation under control. I plan to start on the packet tonight, when we get to the motel in Washington, D.C."

"That's not realistic, Hank," my dad said.

"It'll be after dinner when we get there, and we'll all be exhausted."

"Then I'll start it tomorrow night," I promised. "And I'll do at least half of it." Frankie shot me a look, as if to say, "You're laying it on pretty thick, dude." But apparently, my dad didn't think so.

"Good, Hank, that's what I like to hear. Tomorrow we'll go sightseeing, and then we'll leave the whole evening free so you can do nothing but homework, homework, homework."

Trust me. Any sentence that has the word homework in it three times in a row is not a sentence you want to hear.

I looked over at Katherine. She was just lying there in her crate, sucking down a few more slices of onion. For that minute, I actually envied her. True, she is a lower life form. But then, lower life forms don't have to do homework packets. And that, I thought, was a definite plus for them.

After lunch, we drove about three more hours to Washington, D.C. and checked into the Comfort-For-U Motel. Frankie and I got a room of our own that connected to my Mom and Dad and Emily's. And of course, they wouldn't let us lock the door. We all went to bed right after dinner, because my dad wanted to get an early start the next day. We were going to the Library of Congress in the morning, and he wanted to be full of energy to look through all those dictionaries and card catalogs and other boring things.

As I settled down on my pillow, I thought about how my dad loved books and words and reading and puzzles.

I sure don't take after him was the last thing I remember thinking before I fell fast asleep.

CHAPTER 10

I WOKE UP THE NEXT MORNING totally nervous about my homework packet. I had dreamed that it had arms and legs and a mean, nasty face and was chasing me down a dark alley and yelling, "I'm going to get you, Hank. You'll never escape me!"

While Frankie was still sleeping, I tiptoed to my suitcase and took the packet out from under the pile of underwear. I was relieved to see that it didn't actually have arms and legs. Just a gold clasp and the words HENRY ZIPZER written in Ms. Adolf's handwriting on the front. I tossed the packet on my bed. Well, you have to admit that was a start. It was out. I picked it up. Wow, I had forgotten how heavy it was. I opened the clasp and glanced inside. When I took a serious look at how many sheets of paper were in it, I knew I had to get to work. That thing was going to take me forever and a day.

At breakfast, I actually tried to talk my dad into letting me stay in and skip the Library of Congress so I could work on my packet.

"Hank, the Library of Congress is the largest library in the world," he said. "I think you should see it."

"It has approximately 530 miles of bookshelves," Emily explained.

Oh no, there she goes again. Miss Fact Head.

"Not to mention 29 million books, 2.7 million recordings, and 12 million photographs," she added.

Will someone please stop this girl? Her head is going to explode. She is a danger to herself.

Even though my dad said he appreciated my responsible attitude, he insisted that we all go to the Library of Congress together. And who was I to argue with my dad?

I can definitely say this about the Library of Congress. There are a whole lot of books in that place.

My mom wandered around admiring the architecture and ended up in a section about food and nutrition. My dad headed straight for the dictionary shelves. Emily went with him because, of course, she likes everything my dad likes. Frankie and I didn't know what else to do, so we trailed after them. My dad looked at medical dictionaries, foreign language dictionaries, slang dictionaries, scientific dictionaries, and even an official rap dictionary. I'll bet in that hour, he picked up at least a hundred new words for his crossword puzzle competition. He was as happy as a puppy chasing a stick.

"Look, Hank," he said, practically jumping up and down as he took out a dusty old volume. "A Swedish rhyming dictionary."

"Wow, Dad. That's really . . . uh . . . who even knew there was one of those?"

"You don't see a thing like this every day."

Yeah, thank goodness.

Fortunately, I had a sneezing fit from the dust and I was asked to leave. You know, libraries are very quiet places.

Frankie and I got to wait for the rest of the family on the steps outside. We made up a game to see who could hop on one foot all the way down the steps and back up again. It was way more fun than sniffing dictionaries.

Next, we went to the Air and Space Museum and had a totally great time. We got to touch a real moon rock and see the Apollo 11 command module. Boy, would I love to be an astronaut, except I hear you have to be good in math, which pretty much cuts me out. Oh well. No moon walk for me. But a guy can dream, can't he?

In the afternoon, we went to see the Lincoln Memorial, which is this huge white marble statue of Abraham Lincoln sitting in a giant chair. His foot was as big as my whole body. Emily started rattling off Abraham Lincoln facts, like when he was born and how tall he was, and how many children he had, and blah blah blah blah blah.

In the middle of her boring blabbering, my brain suddenly switched into another gear and remembered something I hadn't thought of in a long, long time. I have never before been able to out-brain Emily, but I swear it happened, right there on the steps of the Lincoln Memorial.

In second grade, during African-American History Month, we had to memorize the famous speech that Martin Luther King, Jr. gave in 1963 at the Lincoln Memorial during a civil rights march. Maybe it was because I was standing right there, but somehow, the whole speech came rushing back to me. I opened my mouth, and out it came. I, Hank "I Can't Remember Anything" Zipzer, stood at the foot of the Lincoln Memorial, just where Dr. King had stood, and said in a big voice:

"I have a dream that one day on the red hills of Georgia the sons of former slaves and the sons of former slave owners will be able to sit down together at a table of brotherhood. I have a dream that my four little children will one day live in a nation where they will not be judged by the color of their skin but by the content of their character. I have a dream today."

I was so caught up in those words that I didn't even notice that a few tourists had gathered around and were listening to me. When I stopped speaking, they all applauded. One man called out, "Good for you, son." My mom was there, too, and had tears in her eyes.

Hank: one. Emily: nothing.

I don't think I'll ever forget that moment

and those words and the way my mom hugged me afterward. If you're ever at the Lincoln Memorial, try it. I promise you will feel really good.

CHAPTER 11

MAN OH MAN, was I ever tired that night. We had been on our feet all day long. This road trip business was hard work.

Back at the Comfort-For-U Motel, I flopped down on the bed in our room and yawned.

"No yawning allowed, dude," Frankie said. "It's homework time."

"I know it," I answered him. The packet was still on the bed where I had left it that morning. "I'm just going to take a five-minute rest before I start."

Frankie was stretched out on his bed, too. He pulled out his book, *Amazing Sports Facts*, and started to read. He must have been really fried, because within two minutes, he was asleep. I mean gone.

I know I had promised to get started on

my homework packet. And I was about to, but sometimes other things get in the way, and well . . .

CHAPTER 12

TEN THINGS YOU CAN DO IN A MOTEL ROOM RATHER THAN YOUR HOMEWORK

1. Lie on the bed and look up at the ceiling.
2. Flip over onto your stomach and bury your face in the pillow.
3. Lie on your right side and look out the window into the parking lot.
4. Lie on your left side and look at the wall with the painting of a sunflower on it.
5. Flip onto your back and check out the smoke alarm on the ceiling.
6. Flip onto your stomach and make snorting sounds into the pillow.
7. Lie on your right side and reach for the TV remote control on the nightstand next to your bed.

8. Flip onto your left side and click on the remote control.
9. Watch the TV screen light up with a whole menu of shows to watch.
10. Think about whether to do your homework packet or watch TV. (Flip the page to find out what I did.)

CHAPTER 13

I'M NOT PROUD OF IT. But yes, I admit it. I did watch a little TV when we came back from dinner at seven thirty.

Okay, five hours of TV. It could have been six.

I didn't mean to watch that long. But circumstances were against me. I mean, how was I to know it was a *Simpsons* marathon night?

When my dad came in to wake us in the morning, the first thing he asked was how much of my homework packet I had done. I quickly pushed the packet off the bed and onto the floor so he wouldn't see it.

"About as much as I expected," I said. As I yawned, I batted the packet way underneath the bed, real casual-like, with my outstretched hand.

"You see, Hank," my dad said, not noticing what I was doing with my hand, "it just takes a little discipline and a little planning, and presto, the world opens up for you."

I glanced over at Frankie and gave him the "don't blow it" look.

"Now get ready, boys. Emily's dying to get to the Science Museum of Virginia."

As soon as my dad was out the door, Frankie popped out of bed and started to pace.

"I'm worried about this, Zip," he said. "How much homework did you actually do last night?"

"Don't sweat it, man. I have this all under control."

"Hey, don't give me that line. I am not your dad. I know better."

"Okay, Frankie. I slipped a little last night. But it was the second night of vacation, and I was in a vacation kind of mood."

"Just remember three words, dude. Colossus Coaster Kingdom. You and me, we're going to ride the Super Duper Looper. And Freefall. Don't mess that up, Zip, you hear?"

Before I could answer, Emily came running in. She was all dressed, with her hair braided and her shoes on.

"Science museum day," she said. "Hurry up and get ready."

"What's the rush?" I asked. "It's not going anywhere."

"I want to have as much time as possible in the museum," Emily said. "The world of science is so fascinating and complex. You just can't spend long enough in it."

"Okay, beat it," I said. "We'll hurry."

While Frankie got dressed, I strolled into the bathroom and found all the little bottles of free stuff they give you in hotels. I love those little bottles. I jumped in the shower and washed my hair with green apple shampoo and conditioned it with a strawberry-smelling cream. I rinsed my mouth with minty mouthwash and finished things off with a peach body lotion. When I was done, I was like a walking fruit cocktail.

"Hank," Emily yelled through the bathroom door. "What's taking so long?"

"A guy's got to be well-groomed for the world of science," I hollered.

"Well, the car's all loaded and we're leaving," she said. "With or without your well-groomed self."

"Where's Frankie?" I called out.

"He's downstairs already. You're the slow-poke."

"All right," I said, opening the bathroom door. "Take a breath, will you?"

"How would you like it if I made you late for the roller coaster park?" she said.

"I wouldn't," I answered. "And don't even think about it."

"Okay, then let's go. I love science as much as you love roller coasters."

You can't argue with a crazed ten-year-old science nut. So I grabbed my jacket, threw an extra bottle of green apple shampoo into my jeans pocket, and ran out the door after her.

CHAPTER 14

SEVERAL HOURS LATER, we pulled up in front of the Science Museum of Virginia. I'm sure I don't have to tell you that Frankie and I were not too excited to be there. I mean, it may have been a thrill for my nerdball sister to spend the morning looking at pictures of atoms and molecules, but for me, I could already feel my brain dozing off. It was only a matter of time before the rest of my body followed right into snoozeville.

To top off the excitement of the morning, as we started to climb out of the minivan, my dad suggested we all bring a pad of paper and a pencil so we could take notes. Well, it was not exactly a suggestion. It went a little something like this:

"Kids, make sure you have paper and a pencil to take notes. I'll review what you've written while we're eating lunch."

"Stanley," I heard my mom whisper to him. "Are you sure we need to go that far? I mean, it is their vacation."

"It's okay, Mom," Emily piped up. "We're here to learn. I've brought a pack of twenty-four colored markers so I can diagram the DNA of snakes, lizards, and other reptiles I love."

"Ah, you must be drawing yourself," I said to her.

"Just get your materials, Hank," my dad said. "Your attitude about learning could be a little more like Emily's."

Emily stuck her tongue out at me, but for the first time ever, I didn't mind. That's because I had a bigger problem than her bumpy tongue wagging in my face.

"Frankie," I whispered in a panic as I rummaged through my backpack, looking for the pad and pencil. "Get over here!"

"Not now, dude. Everyone's waiting for you."

"Look," I said, pointing to the inside of my backpack. "What do you see?"

Frankie looked inside. "A wad of old gummy bears, two broken pencils, a high-bounce ball from a gumball machine, a pad of paper, and a lot of empty space."

"That's what I'm talking about. My home-work packet's not there."

"Oh no. What'd you do with it, dude?"

"What did *I* do with it? What did *you* do with it?"

"Me?" Frankie asked.

"Oh, wait a minute. I never did put it in my backpack. Now I remember. I threw it under the bed when my dad came in this morning. You should have reminded me to take it."

"Hey, stop blaming this on me. You never even told me what you did with the packet."

"Well, I meant to."

"Meant to and doing it are two different things, dude."

"Okay, can we talk about this another time? What do I do right now? It's gone."

"We'll just have to drive back to the hotel and get it," Frankie said.

"And tell my dad I screwed up? No way. Besides, how do I explain to him that the packet was under the bed? Tell me that, smarty pants."

I felt a large hand on my shoulder. It was a hand I knew.

"Come on, Hank. You're holding up the works," my dad said, giving me the Stanley Zipzer shoulder squeeze. He must have learned that from Papa Pete.

"I'll be right there, Dad," I said. "Frankie and I have some important business to discuss."

"There's time for that later," my dad said. "The wonderful world of science is waiting."

And without giving us even a little bit of a choice, he herded us away from the minivan, across the parking lot, up the steps, and into the front door of the museum.

You won't believe what greeted us in the entryway. What you'd expect in the entry of a science museum might be a spaceship or a dinosaur or a huge atom. If it's a really cool science museum, maybe a model of the solar system with the rings of Saturn flashing on and off in neon. But there at the Science Museum of Virginia, what they had in the entry was a gigantic jar of candy.

It was so huge that it almost touched the

ceiling. And it was filled with every delicious type of candy you could think of from all over the world—gummy worms, bubble gum, taffy, caramel, candy bars with coconut, chocolate bars with nuts and raisins, sour tarts, jawbreakers, thin cookie sticks covered with chocolate from Japan, lollipops of every color and one shaped like Switzerland. All I could think of was standing on the edge of the jar, diving in, and eating my way down to the bottom.

"Did we just take a detour and wind up in heaven?" I asked my mom.

She pointed to a big banner over the candy jar. It said, CANDY UNWRAPPED: SCIENCE NEVER TASTED SO GOOD.

"The exhibit," Emily said, "is about the science behind the candy we love. I'm going to use my markers to diagram sugar molecules, both simple and complex."

"Emily, you're my hero," I said. "You know just how to eke out every ounce of fun in any situation."

"Ease up on her, dude," Frankie said. "You've got your own problems."

In the glory of the candy moment, I had forgotten about the missing homework packet. This is what happens to me all the time. I have one thing on the brain, and suddenly it disappears like it had never been there. Without a trace. You'd think that when a guy has lost his seven-thousand-page homework packet, he could keep that front and center in his brain for five minutes. Not me. Not your Hank. My brain was filled with sesame-seed-covered nougats from Thailand.

"Hey, kids, look at that," my dad said, pointing into one of the big exhibit halls. "Have you ever seen a tongue like that?"

In the center of the hall was a giant tongue, as big as the kindergarten jungle gym at our school. Three kids were sliding down the tongue, and as they slid over different sections, the tongue talked.

"Salty, sweet, bitter, sour," it said.

"That's a weird sentence," I commented. Of course, Emily had a comment on my comment. She's a girl who can't resist commenting.

"It's announcing the four flavors the taste buds can actually recognize," Emily said.

"Everybody knows that," I said, which of course, I didn't.

"I don't suppose you know where a butterfly's taste buds are located," Emily said with a smirk.

"I think you'll find them on their feet as well as in their mouths," I answered.

Emily was stunned that I actually knew this science fact. I have to confess, I didn't read it in a book. I saw it on a *National Geographic* special on caterpillars and butterflies. But she didn't have to know that.

Frankie gave me a high five. It was the second time this trip that I got to out-brain my know-it-all sister. In fact, it was such a special occasion, I even high-fived myself.

Emily took off to explore the tongue. Frankie started to follow her because it was a very cool and unusual object, but I grabbed the back of his Yankees sweatshirt and pulled him toward me.

"This is no time for tongue slides," I whispered. "We have a serious problem to solve."

"You keep on saying *we*," Frankie said.

"You're the one with the problem, Zip."

"Fine, I'll solve it by myself. Can I borrow your cell phone? I'll call the motel where I left it."

"My parents gave it to me for emergencies only," Frankie said, "with strict instructions not to make any other calls."

"Look at me, Frankie. Do you not see emergency written all over my face?"

"Okay," Frankie said. "One call."

He reached into his jacket pocket and slipped me his cell phone, just as my dad approached us. I shoved the phone into the back pocket of my jeans, and flashed my dad a big smile.

"Why aren't you exploring the tongue?" he asked.

"Well, Mr. Z., Hank and I wanted to learn all about the taste receptors first, before we actually slid down the tongue," Frankie said, pointing to a list of facts.

"We're trying to take this educational experience seriously," I joined in.

"Did you know, Mr. Z., that the average tongue has ten thousand taste buds on it?" Frankie said.

"That's the number of fans that can fit into the left outfield section at a Mets game," I threw in. I liked the sound of that. My dad did, too.

"It's nice that you boys are taking all this information in," he said.

"Maybe you can use that piece of info in one of your crossword puzzles, Dad. Wouldn't that be something?"

"Speaking of which, I have the crossword puzzle from the Richmond newspaper right here, which I plan to work on while you kids explore," he said. "That's the great thing about travel, boys. There's a new crossword puzzle in every city."

Happy as a baby clam in salt water, my dad strolled off to the coffee bar to attack his new puzzle.

"Okay," I said to Frankie. "Let's go hide behind the tongue and get this call made. I don't think my dad can see us if we sit on the tonsil."

Frankie followed me to the back area of the giant tongue. I thanked my lucky stars that it was plastic and wasn't real, so we didn't have to be dodging spit and already-been-chewed peanut butter patties. That would have been disgusto.

"Dial information and ask for the number of the Comfort-For-U Motel in Washington, D.C.," Frankie said.

As I dialed, I was already panicked, because I'm not good at remembering numbers thrown at me by an operator. I hear them, I repeat them, and I forget them all in the same instant. But I want to say a huge thanks here for the Great Automated Voice in the cell phone, who not only gave me the number, but connected me to it. Thank you, Great Automated Voice. You are a goddess. And I mean that sincerely.

I held the phone up to my ear. The guard at the door was watching us very carefully. I could tell he didn't like the two of us using the tonsil as a phone booth.

I held the phone to my ear. Frankie moved his ear in as close as he could, trying to hear.

The phone rang once. Twice. *Oh please, someone pick up.*

CHAPTER 15

SOMEONE DID PICK UP.

But it was the wrong number.

The Great Automated Voice had given me the Comfort-For-U Motel in Lubbock, Texas!

Great Automated Voice, I take back what I said.

You are not a goddess.

As a matter of fact, you aren't very good at your job.

No offense.

CHAPTER 16

THE NEXT TIME, we didn't let the Great Automated Voice dial for us. I insisted that Frankie handle the whole dialing business. When you're calling long distance, there are a lot of numbers involved, and as I think you understand by now, numbers and I don't get along.

When the person on the other end answered, Frankie said, "Is this the Comfort-For-U Motel in Washington, D.C.?"

I couldn't hear the answer, but it must have been yes, because Frankie handed me the phone.

"The dude talks weird," Frankie whispered, covering the phone so the guy on the other end couldn't hear.

"Weird how?"

"Weird, you'll see."

"Hello," I said, taking the phone and trying

to sound way older than eleven. "This is Hank Zipzer here. You might remember me. We stayed in room 319 last night."

"*Excusez-moi*, monsieur," the man said. "Excuse me, but I do not remember every guest and their particular room number."

Boy, he *did* sound weird. He sounded like Luke Whitman doing his lame impression of a waiter in a French restaurant. I wondered if that accent was for real.

"Trust me, monsieur," I said, giving him back a little of the old French accent, "we were there, and loved your establishment. And now I need a favor."

"That is what I am here for, monsieur," he said. "To provide comfort at the Comfort-For-U Motel."

"I left a very important packet of homework under my bed," I explained. "And I need you to send it to me as quickly as you possibly can . . . as in *now*."

"Now is not good," he said. "Now is lunch-time."

"You don't understand, monsieur. This is urgent. Can't lunch wait a little while?"

"Snails in garlic butter sauce cannot wait. They must be eaten at the precise moment they come out of the oven."

"So I guess a quick peanut butter and jelly sandwich is out of the question?"

"Ah, that is what's wrong with you Americans. You don't understand the delights of a fine French meal dancing across your taste buds, being helped down your throat with an aged wine over a slow two-hour lunch."

"Two hours?" I gasped. "That can't happen. I can't wait that long. Sir, I need you to go to the post office now. I must have that packet by tomorrow morning or . . ."

"Or what, monsieur?"

"Or . . . um . . . America will lose out on who I could have been because my parents will kill me, especially my father. You don't understand, sir, how important it is that I get that packet as soon as possible."

"This is what I mean. You Americans are always hurrying someplace."

"I'm hurrying to become the future of America. Do you want to stop my journey right here?"

"No, I want to enjoy my snails with a crisp garden salad."

I was so frustrated, I handed Frankie the phone and started walking in a circle. Frankie dove into the conversation feetfirst, smooth as only he can be.

"First of all, monsieur, sir," he said. "On behalf of all Americans, and I know this is long overdue, I want to thank you for giving us the Statue of Liberty."

I stopped walking in a circle and just stared at this wonderful dude named Frankie Townsend. What hat did he pull that fact out of? How did he even know the Statue of Liberty was French?

"And second of all," Frankie went on, "let me just tell you that my favorite food, and I know you will understand this, is the french fry—done, of course, the French way."

"Ah, you mean *frites*," the French dude said. I could hear his voice coming from the phone. "Crispy on the outside but soft like a feather pillow on the inside."

"Obviously, you and I understand each other," Frankie said. "And I need you to understand that this is an emergency. My friend Hank has made a mistake, and you and I have the power to help him correct it. America and France, working together. Side by side. Building a better future."

There was a silence on the other end of the phone. Frankie had the guy thinking. Then he went in for the kill.

"Tell me, monsieur, sir," he said with big-time drama in his voice. "With the friendship of our two nations in mind, how can you not go to the post office and mail that packet as quickly as you can?"

I couldn't hear the French dude's answer, but I saw a smile spread across Frankie's face.

"Excellent," Frankie said into the phone. "And what is your name, again? Oh, Pierre Chapeau. That's the greatest name I've ever heard in my whole life. So, Pierre, I guess we're finished now?"

The smile suddenly disappeared from Frankie's face.

"Oh right, overnight delivery is expensive. And certainly, we're prepared to pay for it. Aren't we, Hank?"

"Whatever it takes," I whispered to Frankie. "Just get him to send it. We'll figure out the money part."

"Right, then," I heard Frankie say to him. "Cash on delivery will be fine. Oh sure, of course you need the address." Frankie covered the phone again. "Where should he send it? Where are we going to be tomorrow?"

"Somewhere in Virginia," I answered. "At the bee farm."

"A bee farm isn't an address, dude," Frankie said. "I need a street number, a town, a zip code."

"Keep him on the line," I whispered. "I'll go ask my mom."

Before I could make a mad dash for the gift store where my mom was doing a little shopping, Frankie grabbed me by my Mets jacket.

"Hold it," he said. "I just remembered. I have the itinerary your dad typed up in my back pocket."

Leave it to Frankie to, first of all, know a fancy word like itinerary. (In case you don't know it, it's a list of the places you're going on a trip. I didn't know it either until he told me.)

And second, to have his itinerary with him, where he could actually find it. My dad had made me a copy of it, too, but the last time I saw it was by the vending machines at a rest station on the New Jersey Turnpike.

Frankie read the guy the address of our next stop, which was the Buzz Haven Honey Farm and Snooze Inn.

"Mr. Shampoo," I said, taking the phone from Frankie after he finished giving him the address. "This is so great that you're doing this."

"It had better be, young man," he said, "because my snails are ruined. And by the way, the name is Monsieur Chapeau, as in hat."

"Well, Mr. Hat, you're all right with me."

I hung up the phone and gave Frankie Townsend the biggest high five you've ever seen. This wasn't the first time he had saved my butt, but it was certainly in the top five. There was no time to celebrate, though, because the tallest, strongest man you've ever seen, who was wearing a guard uniform, was suddenly standing over us. Let's just say he was not smiling.

"How would you boys like it if someone sat

on your tonsil?" he asked.

"Now that you mention it, sir, I wouldn't like that at all," I said, jumping off the tonsil like it had caught on fire.

"Hey, guys, there you are!" Emily called out. For the first time in her life, she appeared at just the right time. "You can't believe what's in the next room. It's a lab where you can add all kinds of flavors to 250 different candies. I made a pizza-flavored chocolate bar."

"Hey, I'd love to talk more," I said to the still unsmiling guard, "but we have candy to make. Science can't wait."

We waved a quick good-bye to him. I thought I'd give it one more shot.

"Thanks for the use of your tonsil," I said. "Hope we didn't give it a sore throat."

That didn't make him smile, either. Obviously, the guy had no sense of humor.

Frankie and I ran after Emily to go make candy. After our conversation with Mr. Hat, I felt my problem was solved, and even a pizza-flavored chocolate bar sounded good to me.

CHAPTER 17

IT WAS ALMOST DARK by the time we pulled into the dirt driveway that led to Buzz Haven Honey Farm and Snooze Inn. We could hear a buzzing in the air as we drove up to the main house, which made the whole place seem really eerie. Like maybe swarms of alien bugs had escaped from a horror movie and were hovering in the fields on either side of the car.

Even though it was cold outside, I lowered the window to let the buzz fill the car. Emily freaked out.

"Are you nuts, Hank?" she said, leaning over Frankie and me to reach for the automatic window button. "Put the window up immediately."

"Don't sweat it," I said. "The bees are happy in their hives. They won't bother you if you don't bother them."

"That may be true for one bee, Hank, but we don't know how a colony of thousands of bees is going to react. What happens if they swarm us and I'm stung about a million times and I'm rushed to the hospital but they don't have any anti-bee-sting vaccine? Who will take care of Katherine?"

"Don't worry about it," I told Emily. "We'll turn her loose and her keen iguana instincts will lead her to her relatives in Central America as she sucks flies out of the air with her long, sticky tongue along the way."

Frankie tried not to laugh, but he just couldn't keep it in.

"This isn't funny, Frankie," Emily said. "How can you laugh at the thought of Katherine, alone and abandoned?"

"You're right, Emily, it isn't funny," he said.

Then he burst out laughing again, so hard this time that he sounded like he had the hiccups. I'm ashamed to say (actually I'm not), I joined in.

"Dad, tell them to stop," Emily whined.

"That's enough, boys," my dad said. "Raise the window so Emily can calm down."

By that time, we were in front of the neon sign that said OFFICE. A tall blond man wearing a baseball cap with a yellow and black bee on it came out to meet us. I could see that he also had a bee embroidered on the front of his overalls.

"Welcome, bee lovers," he said. "And if you're not now, you will be when you leave."

"We're so happy to be here," my mom called out. "Aren't we, children?"

The guy didn't seem to notice that no one answered.

"We hope you're going to make yourself right at home here at Buzz Haven. I'm Jimmy Jim James, making sure you have a honey of a time."

He laughed. My mom, who has the best manners of all of us, laughed, too. She reached across the front seat over my dad and stuck her hand out to greet him.

"We're so happy to be here, Jimmy Jim," she said. "I'm looking forward to our honey-tasting tour tomorrow. I try to promote honey usage not only in our home, but in my restaurant, too."

"Then you and me, we're going to be like two bees in a honeycomb," Jimmy Jim said.

"I've put you in rooms 15 and 16. Go make yourselves comfortable. My wife likes to call our rooms bee-autiful. Come on down to the main house for dinner in about half an hour."

"Excuse me, Mr. James, do you happen to have any extra lettuce and maybe a cucumber before dinner?" Emily asked.

"Sure, little cutie," Jimmy Jim said. He must have gone momentarily blind, because of all the things Emily is, cute isn't one of them. "I like to see a young lady who's fond of her vegetables."

"Oh, it's not for me, sir. It's for my iguana."

Emily held up the crate with Katherine in it. Katherine shot her tongue out of the cage. She was going for Jimmy Jim, but luckily she hit the headrest and nearly stuck to it instead.

"Whoa, I'm afraid we don't allow pets here," Jimmy Jim said.

"Oh, Katherine's not a pet," Emily answered. "She's my half sister."

"For a while there, we thought they were twins," I chimed in. "But then Emily grew hair."

Frankie and I cracked up. My father didn't.

"That's enough, Hank," he said.

"I promise you, Jimmy Jim, Katherine travels everywhere with us, and she causes absolutely no trouble," my mom said, still in her charming voice.

"Except when she leaves her droppings on your pillow," I muttered. My dad swung around, even with his seat belt on, to shoot me a world-class "Keep Your Mouth Shut" look. From the corner of my eye, I saw Frankie trying to stuff his fist in his mouth to stifle a laugh, but I didn't dare look at him, because I knew if I did, we'd both lose it.

"Well, I guess if you keep her in the cage, I could make an exception," Jimmy Jim said. "We worry about animals stirring up the hives. You can't bee too careful with bees."

"Bee-lieve me, we'll be careful," my dad snorted, in a rare show of humor. I think you'll agree he's not what you'd call a big jokester.

Our room was number 15. Dad, Mom, Emily, and the unwanted reptile were in number 16.

If I tell you this room was weird, it would be an understatement. It was, as Jimmy Jim James would say, un-bee-lievable. Everything was bee themed. The bedspread had black and yellow stripes. The handles on the bathroom faucets were bee wings. The snacks in the TV cabinet were chocolate-covered honeycomb, orange-covered honeycomb, and honey-covered honeycomb.

What happened to pretzels?

Oh, there they are. Honey covered pretzels. Right next to the bottle of iced tea, flavored with, you guessed it . . . honey.

After we moved our suitcases in, Frankie flopped down on the bed to relax before dinner.

"There'll be none of that," I said to him. "Get your tired butt off that bed. We have a mission to accomplish."

"What now, Zip?" Frankie said.

"We've got to talk to Jimmy Jim before dinner and let him know there's a package arriving for me tomorrow morning."

"Good thought, dude," Frankie said. "We should tell him not to tell your dad. And leave him some money for the delivery."

"Do you think five dollars will cover it?" I asked. "It's all I have."

Frankie took a deep breath, reached into his pocket, and pulled out a twenty dollar bill.

"This was supposed to be for my University of North Carolina hat," he said with a sigh. "But I don't look good in blue, anyway."

"I'll make it up to you, Frankie. I swear."

I knocked on my parents' door to tell them we were going exploring and we'd meet them at dinner. I was worried that Emily would want to come, but she was busy making Katherine a bed out of the cotton balls and Q-tips that were in the bathroom.

"I'm sorry you can't leave the room, Kathy," I heard her saying. "But Mommy's going to make you all comfy and safe."

Could you just throw up?

We headed right to the office. No one was there, but there was a sign over the front desk that said BUZZZZZZZZ FOR SERVICE.

Of course it said that.

We buzzed and buzzed, but still, no service.

Come on, Jimmy Jim. This is no time for you to disappear!

CHAPTER 18

WE WAITED FOR A FEW SECONDS, then buzzed again. Finally, a voice called out.

"Back here, in the kitchen."

Frankie and I walked around the front desk and crossed through the office. We had to be careful not to knock over the bear-shaped and bee-shaped jars of honey that were on display. In back of the office was a big old kitchen. Jimmy Jim was at the stove, standing next to a tall, blond woman who was wearing the same bee overalls as he was.

"Hey, boys, meet my wife, Honey," he said, pointing to the woman who was pulling a big pan of corn bread out of the oven.

"Your name is actually Honey?" I asked. I hoped that didn't seem rude, but the words flew out of my mouth before I could stop them.

"It took me quite a while to find her," Jimmy

Jim said. "I met a lot of Barbaras and Susans, but then one night at the red barn dance, I saw her standing at the punch bowl. I offered to pour her a cup of punch, but when she said she preferred iced tea with honey, I knew she was the girl for me."

"My name was actually Henrietta, but I never liked it much," Honey said. "I had it legally changed to Honey as a wedding present for my Jimmy Jim."

"I hope we're not disturbing you," I said, getting right to business, "but we have something very important to talk to you about."

"It concerns a package coming through the U.S. mail," Frankie said. I could tell he was trying to sound urgent. And it worked, because Jimmy Jim turned away from the frying chicken and faced us.

"Okay, boys, you got my ear. In fact, you got both of them."

"And mine, too," Honey chimed in. "That makes four ears."

"We're expecting a package to arrive tomorrow morning addressed to me," I explained. "It's really important that no one sees that package but me."

"Specifically, Hank's dad, Mr. Zipzer, is not to know about the package," Frankie said. "It's strictly confidential."

Jimmy Jim raised an eyebrow and gave us a suspicious look.

"What are we talking about, boys, that your dad can't know about?"

Uh-oh. Maybe we had overdone it on the strictly confidential bit. I looked at Frankie. He looked at me. And without thinking about it, I blurted out, "Birthday present."

"Right," Frankie said, catching on. "It's a surprise birthday present for our main man, Mr. Z."

Jimmy Jim's face lit up like a Christmas tree. "Now that's what I call considerate."

Honey came over and threw her long arms around my neck. She smelled like a human corn bread.

"If you aren't the sweetest thing, then I don't know what is," she said. "Your parents must be so proud of you. And you, too," she said to Frankie. "I can see why you're best friends."

Okay, I admit I was starting to feel a little

guilty taking all this praise when really all I was doing was covering my butt. But difficult situations call for difficult action. And I rose to the challenge.

"It's something I've been planning for over a year," I said. "I can't wait to see my dad's face when I give him what's in the packet . . . I mean . . . package."

"Can you tell us?" Jimmy Jim asked. "We won't let it out of the bag."

"I'd love to tell you, really I would," I said to them, "but this whole situation makes me so nervous that I really don't trust myself to say."

"He hasn't even told his mom," Frankie said, seeing that I could use some more support. "I'm the only one on the planet who knows what's inside that packet. I mean, package." That was the closest thing to the truth we had said since this conversation started. I felt it was best to get out while the getting was good.

"So not a word at dinner," I said, handing them the delivery money.

"Our lips are zipped," Honey said, making a gesture like she was zipping up her lips.

"I'll keep a lookout for the package tomorrow morning," Jimmy Jim said. "When it comes, we'll bring it to your room wrapped in a towel."

Frankie and I were one smooth team. I was tremendously relieved when we left the kitchen. I promised myself that when the packet came, I'd put it in my backpack and never let it out of my sight again. Mr. Chapeau and the U.S. postal system were giving me a second chance, and I wasn't going to mess up twice.

CHAPTER 19

IT DIDN'T ARRIVE. You heard me. My home-work packet was a no-show.

CHAPTER 20

TEN PLACES MY HOMEWORK PACKET COULD BE

1. In a mail carrier's truck that took a wrong turn in North Dakota.
2. In South Dakota.
3. In no Dakota.
4. Maybe it was coming by carrier pigeon, but thanks to Ms. Adolf, it was so heavy, the poor bird never got off the ground, so he walked back to his home tree and made a nest with it.
5. Maybe Mr. Chapeau never got to the post office, and used the packet as a place mat while he was eating his snails.
6. Maybe the snails actually did the homework, and now they're starting a colony of the world's smartest snails.

7. Maybe aliens who were trying to brush up on their vocab skills stole it and took it to their planet Zork, so their little Zorkians could be bored out of their minds, too.

8. A circus train came upon it and used the pages to line the monkey cages.

9. Now that I think about it, the only thing that homework packet is good for is to catch monkey poop.

10. Seriously, though. Where on earth could it have gone? I don't have the slightest idea. If you see it, please write me. And hurry.

CHAPTER 21

"WE'VE GOT A PROBLEM," I said to Frankie the next morning as I shook him awake. "I just came from the office, and Jimmy Jim said the mail had already arrived. Without my packet. I'm dead meat."

"Breathe, Zip," Frankie said. "There's got to be some way. Let's think this out."

All I could think was that the situation was bad. We were supposed to tour the bee farm, then leave for Charlotte that afternoon. And that meant we'd be leaving without my packet. And that meant I'd have to tell my dad that I lost it. And that meant that he'd have to punish me severely. And that meant I'd never get to ride on the Super Duper Looper until I was thirty-nine and by then I'd be so old, I wouldn't want to, anyway.

So knowing all that, my breathing came to a

full stop. Fortunately, Frankie had an idea.

"Our only link to the package is Mr. Chapeau," he said.

"Let's call him. We have to call him right now."

I grabbed for the phone next to the bed, but dropped it like it was on fire.

"I can't use the motel's phone to make a long distance call," I said. "It'll be on the bill. Frankie, hand me your cell phone."

"Zip, you're killing me. My parents said only for emergencies, and we already had our emergency in Richmond."

"Well if you look up emergency in the dictionary, it will say 'right here, right now.'" I was in full-out panic mode. "And besides, what we had in Richmond was a smallish problem compared to what we have here, which I would call an emergency. No, a disaster. No, a catastrophe. Or whatever is even worse than a catastrophe. I'm begging you, Frankie."

"Relax, Zip. I would've said yes at smallish problem."

Frankie rummaged in his backpack and found the cell phone. We didn't even have to look up Mr. Chapeau's number at the Comfort-For-U Motel, because it was in the memory as the last call we made. I pressed SEND, and after only two rings, that French accent that I was praying to hear spoke up.

"*Bonjour*. Hello. Monsieur Chapeau *ici*. I'm here to help you."

"Oh, I'm so glad you're there," I spat out. "This is Hank Zipzer. Remember me? You were going to send my—"

"Ah, *oui*. Yes, of course, the young man with the homework problem."

"That's me. And the problem hasn't exactly gone away, Mr. Chapeau, because the packet didn't arrive. Not to be rude, but what happened? You said you were going to send it."

"Unfortunately," he began, and I bit my lip hard. I hate sentences that begin with "unfortunately."

"What'd he say?" Frankie whispered, but I held my hand up to signal him to be quiet. I had to concentrate really hard so I could understand Mr. Chapeau's accent.

"Unfortunately, I had an elevator emergency yesterday afternoon," he said. "Some of our

104

guests got stuck between the seventh and eighth floor, and I couldn't leave them. By the time we got them to safety, the post office had closed, so I was only able to send your packet this morning. I'm sure you'll agree I made the right decision."

I didn't know what to say. I mean, I didn't want those people stuck in the elevator, running out of oxygen and screaming for help and water and crackers with cheese and everything like that. But the truth was, I *really really really* needed that homework packet.

"Don't worry, my *petit*, my little one," Mr. Chapeau said. "It will arrive safely tomorrow. Have yourself a nice chocolate mousse and relax."

"Thank you. Thank you so much," I said to Mr. Chapeau, and snapped the phone shut with a little sigh of relief.

"Well?" Frankie said.

"Problem solved, Frankie my boy. The packet will be here tomorrow morning."

"There is only one problem left, Zip. We won't be."

What was wrong with me? Of course we

weren't going to be there. Had my brain gone on its own road trip?

The problem wasn't solved at all. It was right there, as big as it ever was.

There was a knock on our door, and my father's voice shouted in.

"Get ready, boys. I want to be on the road right after we tour the farm."

I sighed the biggest sigh on the entire eastern coast. How do I always manage to get myself into this kind of trouble? I thought I was just tossing the packet under the bed temporarily. I didn't mean to leave it there. I never remember anything until it's too late and I'm in big-time trouble.

"You're going to have to tell your dad, Zip," Frankie said, putting a hand on my shoulder. "We really tried, and we did everything we could. But the game is up."

He was right, I knew it. But the thought of telling my dad that I had messed up once again made all the blood rush out of my head. And besides, I *really really really* wanted to go to Colossus Coaster Kingdom.

All of a sudden, we heard a loud, piercing

shriek coming from my parents' room. It was Emily. And this was no normal "I think I saw a cockroach" shriek. This was a number fourteen on the Scream-O-Meter.

Frankie and I went running to my parents' room. Something was very wrong.

CHAPTER 22

EMILY WAS STANDING in the middle of the room, pointing and screaming. We followed her finger with our eyes and saw Katherine in her crate. She wasn't moving except for her front paw, or whatever you call the front leg of a reptile. That leg was spinning like she was riding a bike. All her other legs were motionless, except this one that was going berserk.

"Something is wrong with Katherine," Emily was screaming.

"You're just figuring that out?" I said. "Something is always wrong with her. For starters, she's ugly."

"Ease up, dude," Frankie said to me. "The girl is upset."

"Look at Kathy's leg," Emily sobbed. "It's twitching."

"Actually, it doesn't looking like twitching to

me. It's more like spinning."

"Hank, this is no time for a vocab discussion," she cried. "What do we do?"

"I don't know. Wait and see if it stops."

"I think this is something serious," Emily said. "I'm worried sick."

"Maybe she was stung by a bee," Frankie said. "I mean, we are in the middle of thousands of them."

"Oh no," Emily said, starting to sob again. "And she's having an allergic reaction. Like Vivian Bell did in third grade."

"I remember that," I said. "Her lip blew up like one of those air mattresses you see on TV."

"Yeah, dude, I thought it was going to explode," Frankie said.

"Do you think that could happen to Katherine?" Emily asked, her voice shaking now.

"I can only hope."

As soon as those words were out of my mouth, I felt bad. I mean, I'm not a big Katherine fan, but I don't want her exploding.

"Sorry, Emily," I said. "I really am. Those words just flew out of my mouth before my brain could put on the brakes."

Just then, my parents came running through the open door.

"What's wrong?" my mom asked.

"We think Katherine might have gotten stung by a bee," I said, filling in for Emily, who couldn't answer because she had thrown herself onto the rug with her face buried in her arms.

"She's going to explode," Emily said through her tears. "Mom, what if she explodes?"

My mom bent down to comfort Emily, and my dad went and checked out Katherine, or as I now was calling her, Katherine the Claw-Spinning Lizard.

"She does look strange," my dad said. "There's definitely agitation in the right front quadrant."

Emily let out another squeak.

"It'll be okay, honey," my mom told Emily. "We'll find a good doctor for her."

"Frankie and I will go ask Jimmy Jim for a vet," I said, and we were out the door before I even finished the sentence.

As we ran to the office, Frankie whispered, "Hey, Zip, this is not bad for us."

"You're telling me," I said, having already had the same thought. "If the vet has a nice long wait in his office, we just might not be able to leave here today. And wouldn't that be a shame—packet-wise."

"Let's hope the waiting room is full," Frankie said. "And the vet is really old and slow."

Lucky for us, he was. Dr. Dexter Phillips was easily a hundred years old, but he had the kindest eyes. You could tell he was a guy who loved animals. He even smiled at Katherine when we brought her into the waiting room of his vet clinic—which, I'm happy to report, was *full* of local Virginia people holding dogs and cats and ducks and chickens. There was even a piglet on a leash that was the cutest little guy you've ever seen. He ran and hid between his owner's legs when he caught sight of Katherine.

"I know how you feel, pal," I said to him, and Emily shot me a dirty look.

While Katherine, Emily, and my mom went into the doctor's office, Frankie, my dad, and I waited outside on the front porch.

"This is a good time for you to bring 'it' up," Frankie whispered to me, while my dad read

111

the *Horse Quarterly* magazine that was on the wicker table in between the rocking chairs. He was probably looking for info for his crossword puzzle clues.

"I'm going in," I told him. I walked slowly up to my dad, and flopped down in the rocking chair next to him.

"Can I talk to you for a minute, Dad? If you want to keep reading, I'll come back later."

"No, what is it, Hank?" he asked.

"I was thinking about Mom and honey," I began. "You know how she loves it so much, and how she was really looking forward to learning all about the different flavors like sage and orange and stuff?"

"Get to the point, Hank," my dad said. I guess he really wanted to get back to that article he was reading on the average length of horse teeth in America.

"Because of Katherine's health issues, Mom never got to take the tour of the honey farm, and I feel really bad about that. And so does Frankie, don't you, Frankie?"

"Down deep bad, dude," Frankie said. What a pal he is.

"We won't be able to take the tour," my dad said. "Katherine's doctor visit is costing us a day, and we're behind schedule."

"My point exactly, Dad. Since we're already here, I think we should stay another day at Buzz Haven and give Mom that opportunity she was so looking forward to."

"If we stay an extra day here, it means we'd have to skip going to Chapel Hill to see the University of North Carolina basketball courts—which was Frankie's choice."

I turned to Frankie. I couldn't ask him to give up his choice, too. I mean, going to see where Michael Jordan played was half the reason he came on this trip.

Frankie was just standing there on the porch. His hands were clenched in fists, his shoulders tense. His eyes looked up at the sky and he took a deep, deep breath.

"I don't really have to see where Michael Jordan played," he said. "I mean, a basketball court is a basketball court, right?"

"Frankie, you would give that up?" my dad asked.

"For Mrs. Z.?" Frankie said. "Are you kidding? She's like my second mom."

"That's really nice of you, Frankie," my dad said.

"Unbelievably nice," I said.

"If you boys don't mind," my dad said, "then we will stay. Randi is going to love this. I think I'll go tell her the good news."

My dad tossed down his magazine and went inside.

"You owe me big-time, Hankster," Frankie said.

"Don't I know it," I answered.

Two minutes later, Emily appeared on the porch with a huge smile on her face.

"Great news," she said. "Kathy's going to be fine. She got a raisin stuck in between her claws, and she was just trying to shake it loose. Isn't she a clever girl?"

This time I had to agree. That Katherine was a clever girl. I mean, how many iguanas do you know who can save you from being grounded for the rest of your life?

Kathy and her raisin claw were my new best friends.

After we returned from the vet's office and

got Katherine all settled down for a nap, we all went for an afternoon tour of Jimmy Jim's honey farm. I learned more about bees than I would ever want to know. For instance, did you know that the average temperature inside a beehive is 93.5 degrees Fahrenheit? And that a bee visits up to one thousand flowers a day to gather pollen to make honey? And that bees fly at about fifteen miles per hour? I didn't know that either, but now we both do.

After the beehive tour, we went to dinner in the Honey Pot, which is the dining room in the main house. Most of the conversation at dinner consisted of my dad asking me detailed questions about how I was progressing on my homework packet, and reminding me that if it wasn't finished, I wasn't going on the roller coasters.

I felt bad because I didn't want to lie to him, but I couldn't really tell him the truth, either. We were about two days past me being able to tell the truth. So I came up with answers to his questions that weren't exactly lies. Like I said, "That homework packet is presenting some really interesting challenges, Dad." Which it was. And, "I'll answer that as soon as I get back from the bathroom." Which I didn't. Or, "My homework packet is just like this honey fried chicken . . . full of flavor and easy to digest." I thought that one was especially clever.

After dinner, Frankie and I started to yawn like sleepy puppies and claimed to be really tired from the stress of Katherine's almost-illness. As soon as we could, we hurried to our room. We told my parents we wanted to get to bed early, but really, it was an excuse to get away from my dad's questions. Even Hank Zipzer eventually runs out of fake answers.

I barely slept, which was good because I was up first thing the next morning. By eight o'clock, I was circling the front desk waiting for the mail delivery. I must have asked Jimmy Jim when the mail was coming at least a thousand times. And when the mail delivery guy finally showed up and pulled that packet out of his bag, I pounced on it like a starving mouse on Swiss cheese. I mean, I clutched it to my chest and hugged it like a long-lost friend. I'm a little embarrassed to tell you, but I think I might have actually kissed it.

"You must really love your dad, to care so much about his birthday present," Jimmy Jim said. "Just give me a hint what's inside there."

"It's made out of paper," I said. "And it's something I've got to finish."

"Oh, a handmade gift," Jimmy Jim said. "Those are the best kind. One year, I made Honey a bee out of saltwater taffy. Brought tears to her eyes, it did."

Jimmy Jim gave my back a nice, firm slap. I know it was supposed to be a sign of affection, but it hurt like crazy. That dude had some strong hands. I flashed him a big smile, trying not to say ouch, and turned to go back to my room with the packet. I hadn't even finished my pivot when my dad appeared at the office door.

"Dad!" I said. "Wow, this is a surprise."

"I came to pay our bill so we can get a nice early start," he said. "I want to be all settled in Charlotte by the afternoon. Tomorrow's the big day."

"Don't we all know that," Jimmy Jim grinned. My dad gave him an odd look, as if to say, "How do you know about the Crossword

Puzzle Tournament?"

"A special day for someone very special," Jimmy Jim went on. I had to stop him before he blew the whole thing wide open. I signaled him to cut the chatter, and he flashed me a knowing wink. I shoved the homework packet underneath my Mets sweatshirt and got out of there.

The strangeness got a little stranger a few minutes later when we were piling our luggage in the car. Jimmy Jim came out of the office to help my dad arrange our suitcases in the back. As soon as the trunk was closed, he turned to my dad, slapped him on the back, and shook his hand like a water pump.

"Many happy returns of the day," he blurted.

My father, who's not exactly a people person anyway, got completely flustered.

"That's very kind of you, sir," he said, "and I'll certainly remember those words on my birthday."

"And we all know when that is, don't we, boys?" Jimmy Jim said, giving us another of his big winks. This called for immediate action on my part.

"Hey, Dad," I shouted from the backseat. "We'd better step on it. You don't want to miss registration."

My dad hopped in the car and put the key in the ignition.

Turn the key, Dad. Put it in gear. Step on the gas. And wave bye-bye to Jimmy Jim, Honey, and the bees.

Wow, that sounded like a rock group.

As we pulled out, I checked to make sure my homework packet was tucked safely in my backpack. It was.

The only thing I had to do was complete it before we got to Charlotte and the Colossus Coaster Kingdom.

No problem. So what if I had a phone-book-size packet of math and reading and vocab to do.

I can handle that. I'm Hank Zipzer, the homework king.

Yeah, right!

CHAPTER 23

MY DAD ESTIMATED the total driving time to Charlotte to be three hours and forty-nine minutes. That didn't count any stops, though, and my mom was planning to stop by the side of the road for a picnic that Honey had packed for us. There was leftover honey-fried chicken from dinner, corn on the cob with Parmesan cheese and honey, iced tea with honey, and for dessert, honey almond cake. And in case we didn't have enough honey, Honey had thrown in an extra bottle of honey to add to any course we wanted.

"We should be in Charlotte by three o'clock this afternoon," my dad said. "That's allowing exactly one hour for lunch, and fourteen minutes for bathroom breaks, which I calculate as two breaks of seven minutes each."

As we all know, I'm no whiz with numbers,

but I definitely got the feeling that a three o'clock arrival wasn't going to leave me much time in Charlotte to complete the homework packet. The best chance I had of finishing it before the next morning was to start in the car.

Frankie and I were in the middle row of seats, and Emily and Katherine were in the way back. Since I didn't want my dad to see that I was just starting the packet, I decided that I had to switch into the way back, where he wouldn't be able to see any of the empty pages.

"Hey, Emily," I said. "Let's change seats."

"No," she said. "Kathy and I like it back here. We're pretending we're princesses hiding in our cave from the fierce fire-breathing dragon."

If there's anything I hate, it's imaginary princesses. But I was a desperate man, so I had to go along with it.

"Wow, Em," I said in a chirpy little voice. "That sounds like fun. But you know, I think the dragon has a good shot to toss a fireball at you through the back window. You'd be safer in the middle."

"Oh, I never thought of that," Emily whispered. "Kathy, gather your things. We're moving."

Kathy, gather your things? Like, what would a lizard have to gather? A cell phone? Or a down jacket with a hood? Oh, I know. Six wilted lettuce leaves and a half-chewed carrot top.

But I couldn't say a word. After all, Emily was making the switch and I needed her cooperation. I kept my mouth shut.

Once Frankie and I were strapped into the backseat, and Emily and her reptile princess were in the middle row, I reached for my backpack. I pulled the packet out, which wasn't easy because it weighed a ton and a half. Then I got a nice, sharp pencil, opened the homework booklet, and turned to the first page, ready to go.

It was titled "Reading Comprehension Exercise #1." There was a long single-spaced paragraph of solid gray type followed by ten multiple choice questions. The paragraph was titled "Magellan Circumnavigates the Globe." Wow. It took me about ten minutes just to sound out circumnavigate, and by the time I was finished, I was starting to get nauseous.

Can I please see a show of hands of any of

you who've tried to do homework while traveling in your family's car? If your hand is up, tell me this. Did you not get unbelievably sick to your stomach while trying to read and travel at the same time? Because let me tell you, as I tried to read while riding in the backseat, I was getting greener by the minute. I don't know if old Magellan ever got seasick, but I sure did reading about him. I didn't even get past the second sentence before I had to yell out, "Dad, stop the car! And I'm not kidding."

"Hank, can't you hold it until we reach a gas station?" my dad said.

"Dad, this is not that kind of stop. And no, I can't."

He looked at me in the rearview mirror.

"Hank, we're on the highway. This isn't a good place to stop."

"Dad, there are only two choices here. Either I barf in the backseat, or you stop and I fertilize the plants along the side of the road."

"Stanley, dear," my mom said. "I think you should pull over right away."

"Yeah, Dad," Emily said. "If he barfs in this car, I'm never getting back in it again. Kathy and I will walk to Charlotte."

"Really, Mr. Z.," Frankie added. "The Hankster is as green as a turtle."

"Actually, there are many species of brown or earth-colored turtles," Emily chimed in, with her usual too much information at exactly the wrong time.

"Well, this particular turtle is about to upchuck all over your ponytail," I managed to get out.

She heard me loud and clear.

"Dad," she said. "Pull over *immediately*."

Which he did. Frankie leaned forward and yanked open the sliding door, which I shot out of like a cannon.

I will spare you the details of what happened next. Let's just say that I didn't realize I had eaten anything red for breakfast.

I didn't try to do any more homework for the rest of the car trip. Old Magellan was just going to have to wait until my stomach left my mouth and went back south to where it usually lived.

CHAPTER 24

OUR MOTEL IN CHARLOTTE had an indoor pool. I saw it when we were standing in the lobby, waiting to catch the elevator to our rooms. Well, I didn't see it all. I saw a sliver of it, but the turquoise blue water was lit up by the last of the sun's rays shining through the windows, dancing on its surface. I could hear the water calling out to me. "I'm over here, Hank. I'm waiting and I'm heated." I had to answer.

"I'll be right down," I said.

"Who you talking to, dude?" Frankie asked.

"The pool. It's calling to me."

"Forget about it, man. That homework packet is calling a whole lot louder."

Frankie was right, and I knew it. I was going to have to buckle down and concentrate for the rest of the day to get that packet done by the morning. I had to keep my priorities straight.

What did I really want to do? Take a swim in an indoor pool or go on seven of the world's fastest roller coasters?

No question about it. The roller coasters won, hands down.

When we got to our room, it turned out to be a two-bedroom economy family suite. The good part about that was that there was a little kitchen, which had a little refrigerator with little bottles of water and orange juice. The bad part was that the bedroom Frankie and I were sharing was right next to my parents' bedroom, and unless the door was closed, my parents could see right into our room. If there's one thing I don't like, it's catching up on an entire week's worth of homework packet while my dad is watching with his wolflike eyes.

That's okay, Hank. You're going to get right to work, anyway. It's not so bad if your dad sees you concentrating. Now go. Ready, begin.

Okay. The first thing I did was put the packet on the desk in the corner of the room. I turned on the desk light, then made sure my pencils were all sharpened and lined up next to the packet. I sat down on the leather desk chair.

Hey, cool. This chair swivels. Maybe I'll just take a few spins around. Yeah, this is fun. Okay, that's enough fun, Hank.

I got myself back into homework mode. I opened the first page and there he was again—good old Magellan. I started to read the long gray paragraph. It was a pretty detailed description of Magellan's ship. Somewhere between the white sails and the tall mast, my mind started to wander. I could feel my brain floating out to sea, just like Magellan.

No, Hank-brain. Do not wander. I command you to keep thinking. Concentrate.

My brain did not listen. So I tried a tactic that works for me sometimes. I stood up next to the chair and put one knee on it. Then I tried reading. Nope, the one-knee position wasn't working. My Hank-brain was still out at sea. So I took my knee off the chair, put my elbows on the desk, and leaned over the paragraph. Then the thought hit me.

I'll come back to this. Magellan can wait. He's on a long trip, anyway.

I took the packet in my hands and started flipping the pages with my eyes closed.

"Frankie, say a magic word," I said. He was flopped on the bed, trying to take a nap.

"Zengawii," he said, as I knew he would. It's the magic word he uses all the time in our magic act.

And as he said it, I stopped flipping the pages, sticking my pointer finger down wherever it landed. I promised myself that whatever it touched was the next thing I was going to tackle.

I looked down at the page. My finger was pointing to a monster of a long division problem. That was no good.

"Say another magic word," I said to Frankie, and started flipping the pages again.

"Roller coaster," Frankie said.

I stopped flipping and looked down at the page. This time, it was a vocab word I actually knew: elongate.

"Definition: to make longer," I wrote.

Okay, one question down. Seven million questions to go.

"Zip, why don't you just sit down and concentrate?" Frankie said. "You've got a lot to do, dude, and all that dancing around is just slowing you down."

Frankie was right. I sat down in the desk chair and put on my serious face. My homework face. My game face. I turned to page seventy-five and stared down at it. It had two columns of words. I was supposed to circle the ones that were spelled correctly.

As my eyes skimmed down the first column, something strange happened. Well, actually not so strange, because it's something that happens to me a lot. The words started to swim around on the page. Not so much swim. More like line dance. I blinked and rubbed my eyes, trying to get the words to stop moving. But when I looked down again, the words were still doing a square dance in the middle of the page.

Why does this always happen to me? Why can't my brain work like everyone else's?

I got up and starting doing jumping jacks. I thought that maybe some exercise would get the blood going and my mind would be able to focus for once.

"Dude, I'm trying to sleep here," Frankie said. "And your butt is supposed to be in the chair."

"It won't stay there, Frankie. I think it's allergic to leather."

"Hank," my father called out. "I'm taking Emily downstairs for a swim in the pool."

The pool! That's a brilliant idea. I'll take a swim, I'll clear my brain, and I'll come back and zoom through the packet.

"Let's go for a swim, Frankie," I said, already out of my chair and heading for my suitcase to find my swim trunks.

"And you'll do your homework when?"

"When we get back. I promise. As soon as we get back."

"I do not want to be going to Colossus Coaster Kingdom without you."

"You know me, Frankie. I'd never let that happen. Ever."

"I do know you, Zip. That's why I'm saying it."

"Fifteen minutes. I'll do a couple of laps, maybe a cannonball or two, and I'll be back on that packet like a bunny on a carrot."

A few minutes later, we were heading down the hall to the elevator that led to the pool. As I stood there in that cramped little elevator, I felt more free than I had in our big bedroom with that packet sitting on the desk. Just being away from the pressure of all those words I didn't know and problems I couldn't solve made it possible to take a deep breath.

The water felt great. It was heated to just the right temperature. I swam and kicked and splashed and dove. When I was finished, I wrapped the towel around myself, thanked the lifeguard, and headed for the elevator to return to the room to finish the packet.

What I hadn't counted on was that there'd be a video game room next to the elevator.

That spelled Trouble with a capital T.

CHAPTER 25

IT WASN'T MY FAULT. After all, the motel had provided a big bucket of *free* tokens. I ran to get Frankie and told him the great news.

"Hey, man, there's free tokens," I told him as he was coming out of the pool. "We can just play and play and play."

And trust me, we did and did and did.

CHAPTER 26

WE GOT BACK TO OUR ROOM LATE, after topping off the evening with melted cheese sandwiches dipped in ketchup in the hotel coffee shop. Well, it wouldn't have been that late if you were a person who didn't have a nine-hundred-page homework packet to do.

Man, was I tired. The drive and the swim and all that concentrating on the video games had taken a lot out of me. On top of that, I moved the packet from the desk to my bed. Big mistake. I had this mental picture of me sitting in bed, under the nice reading lamp attached to the wall, working late into the night, just zooming through the pages.

The problem with mental pictures is that they don't always play out in real life the way they exist in your mind. In real life, there wasn't a lot of zooming through the pages going on. What there was, was a lot of snoring. That's right. I fell asleep, holding the pencil between my fingers, with the packet still open on my lap.

I know what you're thinking. *Hank Zipzer, you're an idiot. Why did you play video games for three hours instead of taking care of business?* That's a good question. And when I have an answer, you'll be the first to know.

When I opened my eyes, it was morning. But the sunlight coming in through the window of our room was blocked by a large figure holding something in its hands. My eyes were still blurry because I wasn't completely awake yet. I tried to close them completely, thinking I was just dreaming, until the large figure spoke with a voice I knew only too well.

"Hank," my dad said. "This packet is completely blank."

"That's not exactly true, Dad. Check out page seventy-four. I knew the word *elongate*."

"That's not funny, Hank. We have to talk."

"I want to talk, Dad. I really do. But that would be very rude, because Frankie is asleep, and if we talk, it will wake him up."

"In the hall," my dad said. "Now."

All the way into the hall, I was trying to figure out a strategy. As you probably know by now, I'm not usually at a loss for words. But at that moment, there weren't a lot of words flooding into my brain or my mouth.

My dad held the packet under my nose.

"Do you want to explain this?" he said.

"Would you believe that I've been trying to complete that packet?" I began. He was silent.

"Okay, would you believe that I wanted to do it? I mean *really really really* wanted to."

"Hank."

"You know, Dad, I understand that you're upset, but really you should be very proud of me, because I have been so creative in ways you couldn't even imagine in pursuing my responsibility of getting that homework packet done."

"The only creative thing I see is all the fibs you told me when I asked you how your homework was coming."

"See, that's the thing, Dad. I wasn't sure when it was coming. Without boring you with all the details, the packet wasn't exactly in my possession at all moments of this trip."

"What are you—"

My dad didn't have a chance to finish his question because the door across the hall opened and a man in his pajamas stuck his head out.

"Are you aware of the time?" he said. "People are trying to sleep here."

"Excellent point, sir," I said, and turning on my heels, I tried to head back into the room. "We'll finish this conversation later, Dad," I said over my shoulder.

Nice try, but it didn't work.

"Come back here this instant, young man," my dad said in a tone of voice that, trust me, you wouldn't have wanted in your face. "I want a full explanation of why your homework wasn't completed."

"Oh, boy, I went through this with my kid," the pajama guy piped up. "I couldn't get him to do a lick of work all through high school. Now he's a brain surgeon."

"See, Dad," I said, grabbing the opportunity. "This is all going to work out fine. A homework packet here or there doesn't make that much of a difference."

"We had a deal, Hank," my dad said. "First of all, this material would have helped you improve your school performance. And second, you didn't keep your end of the bargain."

"Hey, kid, your father has a point," Mr. Pajama Man said.

Wait a minute, buddy, I thought you were on my side!

"But you should go easy on the kid," he said to my dad. "It's almost Christmas. Goodwill toward men. Peace on earth."

"If you don't mind," my father said to the guy, "I don't need a referee. I can handle this matter with my son very well. Thank you, and good night. I mean, good morning."

"Don't mind me. I'm already up for the day," Mr. Pajama Man said. "I won't say a word. I'll just listen."

"And so will I," my dad said. "It's your turn to talk, Hank."

One part of me had the impulse to keep making up excuses. But the other part of me heard Frankie's voice in my ear saying, "You've got to tell him, dude. The game is up."

And since Frankie is mostly right, and to be honest with you, making up all those fibs was really hard work and I was tired of it, I said,

"Okay, Dad, here's the truth."

Mr. Pajama Man reached out and slapped me on the back.

"That's a good kid," he said. "Whoops, I forgot. Not another word. My lips are zipped."

I told the story all in one breath.

"Here's the deal, Dad. I left the packet in Washington. It was missing in action for two days, so Frankie and I talked with Mr. Chapeau and he sent it, but it didn't arrive, and then it did arrive, and then I got nauseous in the car, and when we came here, I went in the pool, and then I saw the video games, which I won by the way, and then I fell asleep, and then there you were."

"Wow, that's some story," Mr. Pajama Man said. "Whoops. I forgot again." Then he zipped his lips.

My dad gave the man a look, then focused his attention on me.

"Do you think these were good decisions you made, Hank?"

"No, I don't, Dad. And if I had to do it over again, I would have handcuffed the packet to my wrist."

"You know there has to be a consequence to this, Hank."

"You're not going to say a sentence using the words roller coaster in it, are you, Dad?"

"I wouldn't, but hey, that's just me," Mr. Pajama Man said. My father shot him a look. "Whoops. You're right. I'll be going now."

He slipped back into his room, letting the door shut with a click.

There was a lot of silence in that hallway for a very long time.

"I'm sorry, Hank," my dad said at last. "I cannot let you go to Colossus Coaster Kingdom. I would be teaching you the wrong lesson. You know in your heart that irresponsibility cannot be rewarded."

I knew that in my heart, but I couldn't control my eyes. Tears started to well up. The one thing I really wanted on this whole trip had just been taken away.

And the truth of it was, it had been taken by me.

CHAPTER 27

As I watched Frankie, Emily, and my mom leave the motel, my heart sank lower than a giant anchor at the bottom of the ocean. I closed my eyes and imagined what their day at Colossus Coaster Kingdom was going to be like. Frankie sitting in the first car of Freefall, his body flying over the roller coaster tracks, his hands waving in the air, his stomach traveling at a g-force of four. (Okay, so I don't technically know what a g-force is, but that's what it said in the brochure.) I saw Emily stuffing her face with cotton candy and hot dogs with extra mustard. I saw my mom waving to them both as they went on every ride in the park.

Even Katherine was going to have a fun day, watching Animal Planet on daytime TV in the motel room.

And then I imagined me, sitting at the Grand

National Crossword Puzzle Championship Tournament next to my dad, watching him and his puzzle pals putting letters into tiny squares *all day long.*

It makes you want to cry, doesn't it?

When we walked into the convention center, it was even worse than I thought it was going to be. There was this big banner that said, Welcome, Crossworders. It was written in squares across and down, like a real crossword puzzle. A bunch of guys in plaid shirts buttoned all the way up to the neck were standing around having a big laugh at the banner. I looked at it again, to see if there was something funny that I had missed. There wasn't.

We entered a big room filled with long tables divided into little cubicles with cardboard partitions. Men and women were sitting in plastic chairs. I don't mean to be rude, but I don't think there was one person in there who had ever thrown a ball. Or had even looked at a ball. They were definitely indoor types.

My dad found a place at one of the tables up front. He picked it so that he could see the large clock on the wall. That way, he could pace himself and finish each puzzle in the allotted amount of time. He was in a pretty intense mood. I tried asking him a few questions about the tournament, and all he kept saying was, "Not now, Hank."

I found a place to sit on the sidelines. I looked around at the tables and chairs. Okay, that took about four seconds. There wasn't much to look at in there. Scratch that. There wasn't *anything* to look at.

A man in a cowboy hat covered with pins sat down next to me. I tried to read what the pins said, but GRAND NATIONAL was all I could make out. He saw me staring at his head, and helped out.

"Pins from the Grand National Championship Tournaments for the last twenty years," he said. "Been in every competition from Omaha to Kalamazoo."

"So you're a crossworder?" I asked.

"The wife is," he answered, pointing to a woman in a matching cowboy hat. "Three-time champion. Twice runner-up. Who you here cheering on?"

"Well, I'm here with my dad, but I'm not

exactly cheering. It more like I'm being punished."

"If he's trying to punish you, then he made a mistake bringing you here. This is even more fun than going down one of them roller coasters, which I did yesterday. This is where the real excitement is."

Was this guy sent here to rub it in? Everyone's been on those roller coasters but me.

Suddenly, a voice came over the loudspeaker.

"Ladies and gentlemen, pencils up. The first puzzle is about to begin. You have five minutes, starting when I ring the bell."

A bell sounded and the room became completely silent. The only thing you could hear was the sound of pencils scratching on paper. I think I dozed off, because when the next bell rang five minutes later, I nearly jumped out of my chair.

The next couple of hours looked exactly the same, as the puzzlers whipped through one crossword after another. Bell. Silence. Bell. Silence. Bell. Silence.

At the mid-morning break, my dad came rushing over to me. He was drenched with sweat, like he had just run a marathon.

"Isn't this great, Hank? The excitement is so thick, you can cut it with a knife."

I guess my knife wasn't that sharp, because I wasn't feeling the excitement. What I was feeling was boredom, but I didn't want to let my dad know that, so I asked him a question.

"So how do you think you're doing, Dad?"

He grabbed my arm and whispered in my ear. "See that woman in the cowboy hat in the second row? She's going to give me a run for the win. She's a three-time champion."

"And twice runner-up," I added.

My dad looked surprised. "How'd you know that?"

"I have my sources."

My dad looked really happy. "So you're getting into the competition, right?"

"Sure, Dad. What's not to get into?"

The guy on the loudspeaker came on again and announced that the competition was about to resume.

"Oh, no," my dad said. "I didn't get my bottle of water."

"I'll run to the snack bar," I said, "and have it waiting for you at the next break."

"You need money?"

"I've got some," I said. I still had a couple of bucks left from the special delivery of my packet. Frankie had paid for most of it, but I had to put some money of my own in, too. My stomach flipped over when I thought of all that I had gone through for that stupid packet.

I gave my dad the water at the next break, and boy did he need it. He must have sweat enough to fill six bottles' worth.

"You're really working hard at this, aren't you, Dad?"

"Your mind, your eye, and your hand all have to work together, Hank. It's a team effort."

"And don't forget your tongue, Dad, because I see it running across your lips when you're concentrating. I do that, too, when I'm concentrating, which unfortunately, isn't all that often."

My dad laughed. Gosh, I like it when he does that.

At lunchtime, we got sandwiches and took them outside. My dad said that the crisp air really helped to refresh his brain. As we ate our tuna sandwiches, made with real tuna and not my mother's tofu-tuna, my dad explained what

145

was going to happen during the afternoon session. The puzzles were going to get harder and longer. And they'd have a theme to them.

"One might be about sports. Another might be about chemistry or George Washington's birthday or capital cities of the world."

"Wow, that's really hard," I said. "The only world capital city I remember is Tegucigalpa, because it sounds like the name of a dance where you shake your hips a lot."

My dad laughed. Whoa . . . twice in one day. Maybe we should declare this date a holiday.

I feel a little weird about telling you this, but by the afternoon, I was really into cheering for my dad to win the tournament. It wasn't quite as exciting as watching a Mets game, but if you let yourself get involved, it wasn't all that boring, either. The person who won the tournament was the one who completed the most puzzles perfectly in the least amount of time.

I was keeping a close eye on the woman in the cowboy hat. She was cool as a cucumber. Not like my dad, who was sweating so much he looked like he had just taken a shower with his clothes on.

In the afternoon, they went through a whole bunch of categories of puzzles. African animals. Famous rivers. The solar system. (Oh man, I hope my dad remembers that Pluto is no longer a planet.) Ancient weapons. (That sounds cool.) And, believe it or not, world capitals. (Go, Tegucigalpa!)

"Hank," my dad said to me as soon as he took his afternoon break. "It was there! An eleven-letter capital of a rain forest country."

"Tegucigalpa!" we both hollered out together. And we danced around in a little circle. The man in the cowboy hat just stared at us.

"Great call," my dad said. "You may have helped me to victory."

Wow. I never thought I'd say this, but maybe deep down, I'm a crossworder.

CHAPTER 28

TOWARD THE END of the afternoon, they announced five finalists out of the three hundred contestants that had started in the morning. The woman in the cowboy hat made it. And so did my dad. The winner was going to be decided based on the last puzzle.

The finalists were up on the stage, and they had to do the final puzzle on their own individual easels while standing in front of everyone. My dad was all red in the face, and his hair was standing straight up, like it does in the morning when he just gets out of bed. He was taking deep breaths and shaking his hands to settle his nerves.

The bell went off, and the five competitors started to write. You never saw markers slide across paper so fast in your life. My eyes started spinning, just watching the letters pour out. I don't think I recognized one word, except for "cavity," which I only knew because it's on a poster across from the chair in my dentist's office.

The final bell rang.

"Finalists, remove your markers from the puzzles," the man on the loudspeaker said. "Since none of you has completed the puzzle, the person with the most correct answers wins."

Boy, if I thought my dad was sweating a lot before, you should have seen him when the judges were judging. His forehead looked like it had a faucet on it. What am I talking about? I was sweating, too. I was really nervous for him.

Finally, the head judge stood up at the microphone.

"Ladies and gentlemen," he said. "It was a close match, but we have a winner and a first runner-up."

I closed my eyes and made a wish. *I hope my dad wins. I hope my dad wins. I hope my dad wins.*

I crossed every finger and every toe. And then I messed up my hair, so that every strand of hair would be crossed, too.

Look at me, rooting for the guy who wouldn't let me go to Colossus Coaster Kingdom. Wow, life is strange.

"The winner is Martina Stone from Cheyenne, Wyoming."

Oh no. It's the cowboy lady. I can't look at him.

"And the first runner-up is Stanley Zipzer from New York, New York."

Hey, they called his name. My hands started clapping and my lips started whistling.

My dad stood up to get his blue ribbon. It looked like he had a smile on his face, but I could tell it wasn't a full stretch of the lips.

When he walked off the stage, I ran over to him and threw my arms around him.

"Congratulations, Dad. You did great!"

"It's only second place, Hank."

"Are you kidding? You got a ribbon and everything. Dad, you beat out 298 people. You're the second-best crossworder in this room. Maybe in the world."

"But I'm not number one."

"You are to me, Dad. I'm so proud of you."

My dad just looked at me. Then he smiled, and this time it was for real.

"You know what, Hank? You saying that is better than the first-place ribbon."

We didn't say another word. We didn't have to. We just walked silently out of the room and to the car. Well, that's not exactly true. When we got to the car, I looked at him and said, "Shotgun."

He laughed and said, "You got it."

CHAPTER 29

LISTEN TO THIS. You're not going to believe it.

Frankie threw up on Freefall all over the couple in the car in front of him. He spent the rest of the day trying to hide from them.

Emily was too short to ride any of the roller coasters. The hot dogs at the snack bar were cold, and they didn't have her favorite yellow mustard.

My mom wound up with two blisters, one on each heel.

On the other hand, my dad and I had one of the most exciting days of my life.

It's a funny thing. You just never know where a good time is going to come from.

About the Authors

HENRY WINKLER is an actor, producer, director, coauthor, public speaker, husband, father, brother, uncle, and godfather. He lives in Los Angeles with his wife, Stacey. They have three children named Jed, Zoe, and Max, and three dogs named Monty, Charlotte, and Linus. He is so proud of the Hank Zipzer series that he could scream—which he does sometimes, in his backyard!

If you gave him two words to describe how he feels about the Hank Zipzer series, he would say: "I am thrilled that Lin Oliver is my partner and we write all these books together." Yes, you're right, that was sixteen words. But, hey! He's got learning challenges.

LIN OLIVER is a writer and producer of movies, books, and television series for children and families. She has created over one hundred episodes of television, four movies, and over twelve books. She lives in Los Angeles with her husband, Alan. They have three sons named Theo, Ollie, and Cole, and a very adorable but badly behaved puppy named Dexter.

If you gave her two words to describe this book, she would say "funny and compassionate." If you asked her what compassionate meant, she would say "full of kindness." She would not make you look it up in the dictionary.